INVINCIBLE SHOVEL

"WAVE MOTION SHOVEL BLAST!" ＝＝＝＝＝★('Д ' ∷)∴ KA-CHOO

NOVEL **3**

GLOSSARY 1

shovel

noun

① Beam Weapon. Acts as a Wave Motion Shovel Blast when heated.

② Refers to a god or something even more divine.

③ A tool that is largely used for shoveling. (Rarely used for this purpose.)

adjective

① Strong, dependable, manly, attractive.

② A condition that the ladies adore, or those actions.

③ Extremely lovely.

proper noun NEW!

① Religious ceremony of the Holy Shovel Faith. All who witness it must perform an anti-madness dice roll (objective: 96). Should the roll fail, they must roll 1d20 and subtract the corresponding SAN points, thereafter becoming a member of the Holy Shovel Faith.

② The High Priestess of the Holy Shovel Faith's unique spell. All who hear it must perform an anti-madness dice roll (objective: 137). Should the roll fail, they must roll 1d20 and subtract the appropriate SAN points, thereby filling the hole in their heart and gaining the Happy Shovel status effect.

verb NEW!

① The act of shoveling a woman's shovel with a man's shovel, thereby shoveling the shovel.
Related → The act of making love.

② Shoveling a young woman's soft, bouncy skin, and experiencing a Happy Shovel moment. This is a religious act.

intransitive verb NEW!

① A shovel so embarrassing than it cannot be written about here.

HOLY SHOVEL EMPIRE, OFFICIAL DICTIONARY (AUTHOR: LITHISIA), 21ST VERSION.

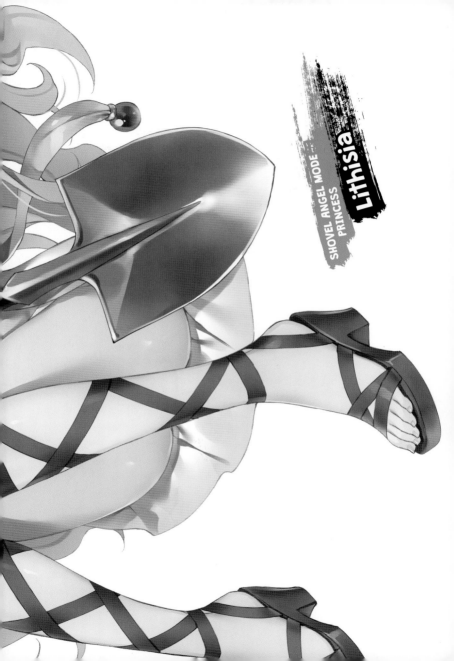

SHOVEL ANGEL MODE
PRINCESS

Lithisia

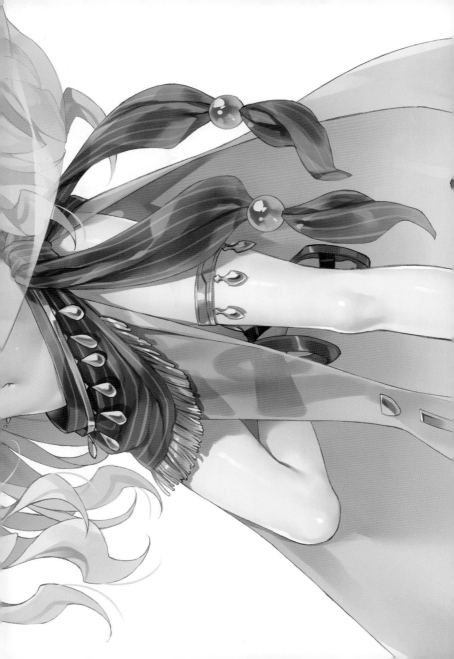

"Eeeek!
No, n-no! The
shovel is coming...!"
—THE IMMORTAL KING ALICE

THE INVINCIBLE SHOVEL

"WAVE MOTION SHOVEL BLAST!"
(´・ω・)σ═════★(ﾟДﾟ；))..∴ KA-CHOOOM

NOVEL
3

WRITTEN BY
Yasohachi Tsuchise

ILLUSTRATED BY
Hagure Yuuki

Seven Seas

Seven Seas Entertainment

Fioriel

The lonely elf

The sole survivor of the elven race. A quiet, kind girl, she has a complex about the enormity of her distinctly un-elven bosom. She resolves to make an embarrassing request of Alan in the name of reviving her village.

"In order to do that, I...I have to do as much shoveling (verb) as possible!"

The young undead king

Alice

Tragically murdered three hundred years ago, she became the vessel for the undead king Veknar. Defeated by Alan, she was meant to vanish, but thanks to the power of his shovel, she was allowed to remain in this world. Every day, she is shoveled by Princess Lithisia...naked.

"All I feel from the sun is a chill."

Lucy

The upstart angel knig

An angel who serves the Sun God. Currently visiting the surface on assignment from God. She meets Alan and Lithisia, and through a variety of happenstances comes to be a Shovel Angel.

"My wings...my wings have been defiled by the shovel!"

The strongest miner on the surface

CHARACTERS

Alan

The strongest miner on the surface, who for some reason is capable of firing a Wave Motion Shovel Blast. Despite having godlike powers, he seems to have no real understanding of how broken they are. He claims he's "just a miner."

"Wave Motion Shovel Blast... DIG!"

Lithisia

The kingdom's lovely princess

A graceful, pure princess on a journey to save her kingdom. She fell in love at first sight with Alan after he saved her from a bandit attack. Has become a self-proclaimed Shovel Princess.

"How Shovely Shoveltastic!"
(Sir Miner's shoveling is incredible!)

he princess's bodyguard

Catria

A young knight aiming to reach the pinnacle of knighthood: a Holy Knight. She puts her position as royal bodyguard on the line by challenging Alan to a duel, only to fail. She grudgingly acknowledges Alan's abilities and secretly finds herself enthralled by his inconceivable strength.

"I'll never give in!
I'll never give in to the shovel!"

In his pursuit of the Green Orb, Alan made his way to the Lactia Republic, where he was framed for kidnapping and duly arrested. With the help of his trusty shovel, he broke out of prison and hunted for the true culprit with his new partner, the noblewoman Lucrezia. Seeing as unearthing the truth is a miner's specialty, Alan was quickly able to deduce that Archon Jistice was the mastermind behind all manner of dastardly deeds.

However, the particular laws of the Lactia Republic rendered a guilty verdict impossible.

"In that case, I'll dig a hole in the law."

"Wait!"

But there would be no waiting. Alan swiftly dug a hole in the law, and in doing so found victory in court with the only piece of evidence he now needed: a shovel. He then dug a grave for the archon and thereby forced him to confess to his many crimes. On the battlefield of the courtroom, the shovel was the ultimate weapon.

In fact, the shovel was so strong that Alan was also able to effortlessly unearth all of Lucrezia's dirty little secrets.

"Wait, no, no! Don't look! Don't loooook!!!" (*Please refer to the image on the left.)

Meanwhile, Princess Lithisia's public shoveling of Alice, a semi-naked young woman, allowed her to corrupt the Lactia Republic with shovels, hastening her Human Shovelmentality Project. At last, the miner and princess's journey took them to the open seas in pursuit of the next orb.

Someone, for the love of all that is holy, please stop them.

—ADAPTED BY: A REALLY HARD-WORKING ALICE

SCOOP MUSO VOL.3
「SCOOP HADOHO!」(` · ω · ´)♂＝＝＝＝★(° Д ° ;;;).:·. DOGOoo

©Yasohachi Tsuchise 2019
Illustrations by Hagure Yuuki

First published in Japan in 2019 by
KADOKAWA CORPORATION, Tokyo.
English translation rights arranged with
KADOKAWA CORPORATION, Tokyo.

Seven Seas press and purchase enquiries can be sent to
Marketing Manager Lianne Sentar at press@gomanga.com.
Information regarding the distribution and purchase of
digital editions is available from Digital Manager CK Russell
at digital@gomanga.com.

Follow Seven Seas Entertainment online at
sevenseasentertainment.com.

TRANSLATION: Elliot Ryoga
COVER DESIGN: Nicky Lim
LOGO DESIGN: George Panella
INTERIOR LAYOUT & DESIGN: Clay Gardner
PROOFREADER: Kelly Lorraine Andrews, Stephanie Cohen
LIGHT NOVEL EDITOR: E.M. Candon
PREPRESS TECHNICIAN: Rhiannon Rasmussen-Silverstein
PRODUCTION MANAGER: Lissa Pattillo
MANAGING EDITOR: Julie Davis
ASSOCIATE PUBLISHER: Adam Arnold
PUBLISHER: Jason DeAngelis

ISBN: 978-1-64505-826-7
Printed in Canada
First Printing: December 2020
10 9 8 7 6 5 4 3 2 1

CONTENTS

Catria's Sea Log

CATRIA DECIDED TO KEEP A LOG aboard the Ultimate Shovel as it sailed across the ocean. A sea log, if you would. Normally, this was a captain's responsibility; all nations required a ship's record of travel prior to entry. However, upon reviewing the captain's log, Catria discovered only the following words: "Day One. The shovel shoveled."

Given that Lithisia was the captain, what else could the lady knight expect?

"I...I have to do something!" And so Catria took the responsibility on herself. "You can do it, Catria! You've got this! You must be the keeper of common sense!"

Filled with gusto, Catria took up her quill pen so that she might hold down the proverbial fort. She proceeded to document the last three days of travel.

MONTH X, DAY X. WEATHER: SUNNY

First day on the open ocean.

In search of information regarding the legendary orbs, we left the Lactia Republic. We're headed east, moving at three times normal speed using the ship's Shovel Sails. We were beset by a fierce storm, but with crewman Alan's Wave Motion Shovel Blast, we were able to blow it away. Thanks to him, the weather today is bright and sunny.

"I can't do this," Catria muttered.

But she knew she had to be honest about what had transpired. Putting lies to paper went against her chivalric code as a knight. Thus, Catria continued to write the log that had already been defiled by the wicked shovel.

MONTH X, DAY X. WEATHER: SUNNY

Second day on the open ocean.

The new sails are tremendously effective, and our cruising speed is astonishing. The ship has begun to sail above the surface of the water. According to crewman Alan, this is a result of the "Shovel Skipping Effect." This effect enabled us to break through the difficult shallows known as the "Radical Lacteal Seas." As such, we've managed to cut our total travel time in half.

"I can't. I just can't."

Regardless, Catria could not pen falsehoods. A knight could not lie. Despite feeling like she was regressing in age and brain power, she continued to write.

MONTH X, DAY X. WEATHER: SUNNY

Third day on the open ocean.

We ran across a fleet of seven galleons, which opened fire on us. Crewman Alan shielded the ship with his Shovel Barrier, then with his Shovel Vaulting (you get the idea), single-handedly boarded and captured the enemy galleons.

Per order of Captain Lithisia, we tied up their crews for Shovel Interrogation, whereupon we discovered they were a private fleet from neighboring Elessaria. Captain Lithisia ordered us to engage Elessaria and their Invincible Fleet of 718 Ships in battle at sea.

To bolster our forces, crewman Alan assembled a fleet of Wave Motion Shovel Blast Ships (718 of them). Needless to say, they were Shovel Ships. Following a massive shot comprised of every Shovel Ship's Wave Motion Shovel Blast, the opposing fleet was sunk. We even captured Princess Elias, who was leading Elessaria's fleet. Lithisia interrogated her personally.

This battle was officially christened the "Great Shovel Sea Battle," and a grand "Shovel Feast" was held aboard our ship, bringing us to the present.

"..."

Catria placed down her quill and raised her head. "I wonder if they're still going at it up there..."

"Sho-vel! Sho-vel! Sho-vel!"

Rough voices chanted on the deck of the Ultimate Shovel, audible even in the captain's quarters. The crew was still enjoying their little Shovel Feast. At the center of it all, Captain Lithisia was shoveling Princess Elias (something one ought never do to an enemy princess).

Alan, on the other hand, had gone out of his way to save the crews of the ships he had sunk into the ocean.

"Hi, everyone! Here's the evil princess who caused you all so much pain and suffering! Scoopy doopy scoop time!!!"

While Alan saved his fellow humans, Princess Lithisia was having her way with the enemy princess on the deck of their ship. In fact, Catria had dedicated herself to writing in the captain's log in order to flee from this very scene.

"P-please! Have mercy! N-no more shoveliiiiiing!!!" Princess Elias was a sixteen-year-old blonde beauty. The once domineering princess was now crying for mercy in a pathetic wail.

"Scoopy doopy, shovely wobley!"

"EEEEEEK!!! WHY ME?! I HAVE NOTHING TO DO WITH THIS!!!" Alice had unfortunately also been dragged into this little debacle.

"Perfect." Meanwhile, back in the captain's quarters, Catria laid down on the bed. It was no good. She could no longer hold out. "I'm just...gonna sleep now."

Catria gave up on the world and decided to hunker down and wait for Alan. From the very beginning, this journey had been a problem, a disaster, just no good. No good at all.

Ring of the Archangel
Equipment: Accessory

RARITY
SR (Shovel Rare)

EXPLANATION
A heavenly treasure inlaid with the precious gemstone "Eljarir," imbued with the magical power of the Sun God, El. Only angels of Rank 3 or higher (as represented by the Shovel Triangle) can equip it. Its form is extremely shoveltastic.

SPECIAL EFFECTS
① The right to command all angels below Rank 6.

SECRET
This ring has a secret. Normally, only the above text appears when this item is examined. However, when examined using "Shovel Appraisal," the text below is revealed.

HIDDEN EXPLANATION
This ring has been corrupted by Shovel Power. Its true name is the "Heavenly Shovel Ring." In addition to its usual effects, it also grants the following.

HIDDEN SPECIAL EFFECTS
② Shovel Corruption of Words: The words "shovelly" and "shovel" naturally become a part of the wearer's language.
③ Shovelsation Corruption: Will now become aroused by the shovel.
④ Shovelnoia: Any who equip this ring for more than seventy-two hours will fall deeply in Shovel Love with the ring, wanting to never part with it. Even after removing the ring, if one does not have "Brainwashing Resistance," "Shovel Resistance," or "Madness Resistance," this effect will last for all eternity.

HOLY SHOVEL EMPIRE, OFFICIAL DICTIONARY (AUTHOR: LITHISIA), 21ST VERSION.

CHAPTER 6

Shoveling the Mermaid Nation

PART 28

The Miner Saves Lala, the Mermaid Girl

ALAN STOOD ON THE DECK of the Ultimate Shovel as waves murmured against the hull. With him stood the noblewoman, Lucrezia; the lady knight, Catria; and of course, the captain, Princess Lithisia.

"Our voyage is right on schedule."

They were now several weeks at sea, northeast of the Lactia Republic, quite far from the mainland. All around, they could see nothing but for the vast ocean stretching out in every direction. Furthermore, they were in an area frequently struck by fierce storms where ships often met their end. As such, it wasn't a trade route, and ships rarely ever charted their voyage through it.

It was, in other words, a part of the ocean largely untouched by humanity. At the center of it all, Lucrezia explained, was the mermaid paradise, "Mermaid Oasis."

Being the daughter of a merchant, Lucrezia knew quite a bit about the ocean.

"Mermaids, eh? I had no idea they really existed..." Catria said.

Sure, she knew about demi-humans that resembled animals, but to Catria, mermaids were mythical creatures. She knew them as beings skilled in song and had heard legends that humans who received a mermaid's blessing were able to move beneath the ocean's surface with no trouble at all. It was also said that consuming a mermaid's flesh would grant immortality. A dubious tale at best.

"But I guess at this point, it'd be weirder if they didn't exist."

After all, a man who could fire a Wave Motion Shovel Blast from his shovel was standing next to Catria. At this point, mermaids were nothing.

"According to my father, there is a set of ruins sunk deep within the Mermaid Oasis," said Lucrezia.

That was likely the location of the Green Orb.

"Deep within, eh?" said Alan. "Hrm. How are we going to get to it?"

A voice cried out from the crow's nest, causing everyone on deck to tense. "Thar be the shallows! That's gotta be the Mermaid Oasis! All crew, Shovel Salute!"

The thunder of the ship's whole crew running up and stabbing their shovels into the deck filled the air. In an instant, the crew was lined up in a row with their shovels positioned before them. As one, they used both hands to form a triangle; a strange pose indeed. This was their way of saluting the shallows. They didn't move a muscle beyond that.

"Princess, what's going on?"

"You don't know, shovel? My dear Catria, to think you lack common knowledge of proper conduct on the sea."

"I'm of the opinion that you're the one who lacks common sense, Your Highness."

"What you're looking at is diplomatic courtesy. We're paying our respects to the mermaids. By stabbing our shovels into the deck, we express that we have no ill intent. By greeting them with the shape of the shovel, we show that we come in peace. This is the respectable way to signal amicable relations upon the open seas."

This greeting would be entirely meaningless to someone not of the Holy Shovel Faith.

"Um, you guys are destroying the deck with your shovels, though."

"It's fine. I shall welcome all the mermaids into our marvelous religion! The holes in the deck will be filled in due time."

What in the hell is she talking about? cried Catria deep within her heart of hearts. "Alan, please do some...Alan?"

"This is bad..." Alan whispered to himself. His line of sight was fixed on the shallows in the distance, which were just barely visible. That said, Alan's eyesight was far, far above average. He could spot a gemstone up to ten miles away. "I can see a mermaid, but...they're being attacked by hawkmen."

On one of the submerged rocks jutting from the shallows cowered a small mermaid girl. She was surrounded by four or five monsters, hawkmen, wielding harpoons. She appeared to be alone.

"Then it's time for your trusty Wave Motion Shovel Blast!" said Lithisia.

"No, the rock is too small. If I dig a hole in it, she'll fall off," said Alan.

"You could always...not dig a hole?" said Catria.

"Then how could he ever call himself a miner? Catria, are you out of your mind?"

In that instant, Catria received the greatest shock of her life: the princess doubted her sanity.

"Then let's fly, Sir Miner!"

"No, that won't work. Because of the terrain effect on the Ultimate Shovel, my Shovel Power is too strong. If I try to fly, I'll create a sonic boom that will destroy the ship."

"I'd argue destroying this ship would be for the better-ment of humanity," muttered Catria. But her comment was swallowed by the empty sky.

"I'm going to use the Shovel Rifle this time," said Alan.

"Wait, isn't that the thing that turns the ground into bullets?" asked Catria.

"Correct."

"We're on the ocean."

"Sure are." Alan raised his shovel and leapt down from the bow of the ship. At the same time, he slapped one of his extra shovels on the ocean surface. Then, just like on the snowy mountain of the ice nation Shilasia, the shovel expanded in width and length until Alan could surf atop it.

"That's Sir Miner's Water Shovelboard!" Lithisia explained as her voice sparkled with joy.

"Your Highness, did you just come up with that excru-ciatingly lame name?"

"No, Catria. It was a name given unto us by the heav-ens above. Truly a shovel fit for the sea!"

Someone remind me why I work for this woman...

Just as Catria tipped into an existential crisis, the mer-maid's cries echoed across the shallows.

The mermaid was still a child, and her expression was that of despair. She was on the verge of being kidnapped by hawkmen and there was no one to save her. Her eyes cried out for help: *I'm scared! Don't come any closer! Someone save me!*

Those who sought salvation would be saved. That was the miner way. Alan skidded ever closer on his Shovelboard, waves flying in his wake.

"If there's no ground..." Alan once again raised his shovel and focused his energy into it. "DIG!"

KA-CHOOOOOOOOM!

He directed his Wave Motion Shovel Blast at the ocean itself. His beam dove deep beneath the surface—a thousand feet deep, to be specific. The width of the beam grew to many thousands of times more than the radius of the shovel, making the ocean look like a giant stake was sticking out of it. In the end, the Wave Motion Shovel Blast's total diameter exceeded one mile, breaking the ocean in two.

The mermaid gaped in shock.

The hawkmen gaped in horror.

Lithisia clapped in delight. "Shovelmazing!"

Catria was empty of any emotion.

Thanks to the Wave Motion Shovel Blast, everyone could see the seafloor.

Alan nodded in satisfaction. "Perfect, there's the some good earth down there. Bullet fodder aplenty."

Three! Alan threw his shovel down and scooped up some dirt.

Two! Alan fired his Shovel Rifle at the hawkmen, but the shocked monsters were frozen in place.

One! Kathunk, BOOM.

In three seconds, the hawkmen had been annihilated. While this happened, the mermaid girl stared, jaw hanging, at Alan, her expression utterly still.

Alan turned over his shoulder and called back to the ship. "Catria, never forget..."

"What now?"

"You implied I wouldn't be able to use the Shovel Rifle above water, no? Well, you see..." Alan adjusted the shovel in his hands. "When it comes to nautical combat, the shovel is the most powerful weapon in the world."

Catria let out the greatest sigh of all time. As she stared at the giant hole in the ocean Alan had created with his Wave Motion Shovel Blast, she thought to herself, *I'm not sure this qualifies as nautical combat anymore.*

The mermaid girl sat unmoving, her mouth fixed wide open. Catria really felt for her.

"Kweh?! Kweh, kwehhhhh!!!"

They carried the mermaid girl back to the Ultimate Shovel and treated her with Shovel Healing, which somewhat lessened her confusion. Nonetheless, she looked at Catria and the others with tears in her eyes and made a trail of sad, sweet noises. She was quivering in fear. On occasion, she looked overboard at the ocean and moaned, "Kweh." She clearly wanted to escape over the edge and flee, but they were so high up in the air that she was scared.

"My father was able to communicate with mermaids via a treasure known as 'Mermaid Tonic,'" Lucrezia explained apologetically. Unfortunately, she didn't have any on hand. "This will be a problem. We must ask her where the ruins are."

"Don't worry, Lucrezia. I have a shovel."

"Excuse me?"

Alan gingerly tapped his shovel against the deck of the ship. Just like that, walls rose up, surrounding the mermaid. The wooden walls were inscribed with a morass of letters and characters in different languages. When Alan knocked on one of the walls, a large hole opened in it.

The mermaid girl continued to shake in fear. "No, please! No eat! I taste no good!"

Alan smiled at her. "Hey there, don't worry, no one's gonna eat you. I promise."

The mermaid girl started. "Eh...? You understand mermaid...?"

"That I do. My name is Alan. What's yours?"

The mermaid girl summoned her courage and met his eyes. "Lala..."

"Lala, eh? Well, I took care of those nasty hawkmen. You're safe now."

Lucrezia watched Alan and Lala converse with a puzzled look on her face. "Alan, what exactly did you do?"

"Just poked a hole in the wall that is language. Nothing to it."

"'That's all' my foot!"

Having Lucrezia around sure does take some of the straight-man burden off of me, Catria thought as she gazed with relief upon the only other sensible human on the ship.

Meanwhile, Lala remained altogether bewildered by her predicament. "No eat me?"

"Nope, and that's a promise. I'll have you know a miner's favorite food is jewels, not mermaids."

"That's silly... Hee hee."

Alan's dumb miner joke went over well, and the mermaid girl giggled. She fanned her tail and bowed her head deeply. "Thank, Alan. I owe you, gratitude."

Due to the Shovel Translation, her sentences were a bit spotty, but the meaning got through just fine. The tense atmosphere finally faded.

Alan shook his head. "No need for thanks. Any shovel wielder would've done the same."

"Shovel...wielder? Humans, amazing!"

"He's not human," said Catria.

"Yes, I am. This lady knight right here, Catria, can do what I did, too."

"I will never shovel a thing!"

As they descended into banter, Lucrezia interrupted with all the genteel grace she possessed as a noble. There was nothing wrong with a cozy little chat, but there was a great deal they needed to learn from this girl. "So, Lala. Do you have any mermaid friends?"

Lala turned in on herself, eyes on her hands. She whispered, voice frail, "They taken...away. All but me."

"Taken? By who?"

"Lernia Hydra." Lala cast her gaze across the ocean. "The master of ocean. I could, never defeat, that."

Tears gathered in Lala's eyes, sliding down her cheeks. But before they hit the deck, Alan caught them with his shovel. "Understood."

"Eh...?"

"So we just gotta beat that Hydra thing, right?"

The mermaid girl blinked rapidly and frowned up at Alan. She clearly couldn't believe what she was hearing. "Alan...Alan, can't! We...different."

"How so?"

"You are of land. I am of ocean." Lala shook her head. "Those of ocean mustn't rely on those of land. Must settle own matters. Rule of ocean."

This was likely some manner of mermaid rule put in place to protect the independence of their species.

"Well, it's too late for that," said Alan. "I already saved you from the hawkmen, didn't I?"

"Y-yes, but...well..."

"Plus, I'm a miner. I'm a man of the ocean."

"Eh...? Alan, two things, not connected."

"The land and the ocean are absolutely connected. Deep at the bottom of the ocean is the ground. And that means..." Alan pointed his shovel at the surface of the water. His gaze descended far below, into the depths. "The ocean floor is also a shovel battlefield."

Catria sighed as she looked at Lala, whose mouth was once more wide and gaping. Catria knew all too well there was no such thing as a non-shovel battlefield.

PART 29
The Lady Knight Fires Her (Self-Proclaimed) Holy Wave Stream

ACCORDING TO LALA, they needed to reach an underwater ruin some thousand feet beneath the ocean's surface. The ruins were once a glorious shrine to the god of the sea, Lernia Hydra. In those halcyon days, the shrine was a paradise for mermaids and other demi-humans.

But a few years ago, humans had brought a strange orb that swiftly turned the shrine into a den for monsters. Prime Minister Zeleburg was likely behind this heinous act.

Lucrezia's father had sealed the shrine door in an attempt to keep the monsters trapped inside, but considering the hawkmen who had menaced Lala, the door might well have been opened.

The party hoped to find the kidnapped mermaids within the shrine as well.

"Then let's be on our way," said Alan. "Catria, you're with me."

"For real?"

"Didn't I promise to train you into a full-blown Holy Knight?"

Alan had indeed promised her that. All the same... Catria turned in a slow circle.

She found Alice fishing off the bow of the ship. It appeared as though the Undead King had grown weary of the haunting shovel atmosphere and was indulging in some dedicated escape from reality. Lucrezia, on the other hand, looked like she wanted to join the underwater journey, but the trip would be too dangerous for a normal human such as herself. Once they found the seal that could only be opened by one of Lucrezia's lineage, they could bring her down with Shovel Dive.

Catria wondered if they could switch places. And yet.

"Let's go." Alan hefted his shovel, primed and ready to dive into the ocean.

"Whoa, wait!" Catria waved her hands in protest. "How the heck am I supposed to swim a thousand feet below the ocean?!"

"Come on, that's simple. You dig up the oxygen present in the water using Shovel Breathing. It's one of the basics of clearing an underwater dungeon."

"You're the only human on this planet who could pull that off."

"Catria, don't play around. Just do it."

"I can't do the impossible!"

"Wait, Alan!" Lala crawled over to Alan on her fishy tail. She looked terribly concerned, as she still couldn't believe he was going to face the Hydra. She anxiously waved her tail as she clenched her fists and pleaded with the miner. "Alan, you no have fins! You can't dive, into ocean!"

"Don't worry, Lala," Lithisia cut in. "We don't have fins, but we do have shovels."

"Shovels not fins!"

"Now that's simply incorrect. A shovel is about 90 percent fin. Take a look." Lithisia brought over a shovel from the corner of the ship's deck. It wasn't Alan's sword-tipped shovel, but rather one with a square head. Lithisia popped off that metal head and placed it against her butt, flapping it around. "See? Shovels can become fins!"

"Whaaa?!"

"Lala, not too long ago you said the two of us were different. Humans and mermaids, those of us who live on land and those who live beneath the sea... And you're right, we *are* different. Our bodies, hearts, and where we live, none of these are the same. But even so." Lithisia smiled. "Even so...as long as we have shovels, we can understand one another."

Lala blinked at the princess, then her eyes sparkled. "We...can?"

Like hell, Catria thought to herself as her own eyes darkened. This stupid princess was corrupting even an innocent mermaid with her shovel religion nonsense. Did this qualify as marine pollution?

"I no really understand, but okay. I no stop you..."

"Mm."

"That's why, I do what I can. Alan, raise head."

"Hrm?" Alan looked questioningly at her.

What was Lala planning? For now, he crouched down and held his head like she asked. As he did, Lala brought her mouth close and blew into his. Something whooshed from between the mermaid girl's lips into Alan's, and with that she pulled away.

"..."

Alan remained crouched for a moment, lips parted in surprise. Lithisia, on the other hand, was frantically opening and closing her mouth like a baffled fish.

Lala was the only one still moving. Her cheeks glowed in high color. "Mermaid kiss... It bring you great, fortune."

Suddenly, a glimmering membrane wrapped around Alan's head. It swelled up like a soap bubble, then formed into a kind of transparent helmet. Lala went on to "kiss" Catria as well, resulting in the same membrane appearing around her head.

"Oho!"

"Alan, now you breathe underwater. Yours last about three days. Catria's last three hours. This due to difference in adaptability."

"That's no good at all," said Lithisia. "Catria, hurry up and abandon your humanity, please."

"No, thank you!"

Lala turned to Alan once more and nodded once in gratitude. "Please, Alan. Save mom, dad, and, everyone."

It was an honest request, and Alan wasted no time pursuing it.

He hopped over the edge of the Ultimate Shovel and began to furiously dig through the water at high speed. Behind him, Catria clung onto his legs, and Lala followed up with her elegant underwater maneuvers. In the very back was Lithisia, whose dress had transformed into a frilly bathing suit.

Of course, this suit was a rather seductive white two-piece. While the color scheme emphasized Lithisia's "purity," the lack of overall cloth brought ample attention to the swell of her breasts. She exuded a sensuous aura befitting a Shovel Princess.

Incidentally, Catria had also donned new underwater gear. For some reason, Lithisia had prepared a rather tight-fitting blue sports bathing suit for her. Who knew what she was thinking when she readied it.

"Hold on, Your Highness!" Catria had realized something was very off. They were already two hundred feet deep. "How are you following us? Lala didn't 'kiss' you, did she?"

"Ah! I forgot! You okay?!" gasped Lala.

"Of course I'm fine! I'm using Shovel Breathing. It's simple." Lithisia held the grip of her small red shovel in her mouth. She was sucking up air through the open space of the handle. The head of the shovel produced white bubbles that entered her mouth. If one listened carefully, they could hear her breathing sounds: "Shoo, velll. Shoo, velll."

This stunning revelation nearly caused Catria to pass out.

"Lithisia, that's an ability called Snorkashoveling," said Alan. "Not bad. Not bad at all."

"Scoop you so much, Sir Miner! Also, um...how's my bathing suit?" Lithisia squirmed as she shyly squeezed the head of her shovel between her breasts. This further emphasized their largeness and softness as they wafted with the current of the water. She pressed her thighs together too, making for quite the attractive sight.

To put it mildly, she was alluring as all hell.

"Do you...like it?" Although Lithisia was bashful, she was extremely invested in Alan's answer.

But from the blank expression on his face, it was clear he didn't really get what she meant.

She pressed, "Um, um... When I wear a bathing suit like this, do you think I'm a 'shovel'?"

"Er, I'd argue you're plenty 'shovel' all the time."

Upon receiving this answer, tears welled in Lithisia's eyes (even though she was underwater). "Ah... Aaaah... I'm so shoveled (shovelly moved)!"

"Enough with the shovel words!"

"Catria, humans amazing," Lala said, endlessly impressed by the party.

Catria shook her head. It was hard, scientifically provable fact that these two were no longer human.

The party continued to plow through the water at explosive speed. Soon, they saw a giant something-or-other shining green in the distance. It looked similar to Rostir Castle, but was in fact far larger. It also emitted an astronomically oppressive aura, as if the castle itself were a giant monster.

That's the Deep Sea Shrine?! thought Catria.

"Lala, is that where the kidnapped mermaids are?"

"They captured in underground prison. I can't get in by myself..."

Suddenly, a strange voice found its way into the party's ears. "R-run away...run...you mustn't come here, Lala!"

"Mommy?!"

The voice was unclear at first, but it soon grew more understandable. Gradually, the form of a beautiful translucent woman took shape directly in front of Lala. She closely resembled the young mermaid; it was obvious this was Lala's mother, and that she was using some kind of long-distance telepathic magic to project herself.

"Mommy, Mommy! I here, save you! I bring strong, people!"

"No, Lala! You mustn't come! Run away! Hydra is..."

"Don't worry! Alan strong! Shovel strong!"

Alan nodded. "Indeed, ma'am."

"Who are you...?"

"Alan. Alan the miner." Alan gripped his shovel as if this explained everything.

But Lala's mother shook her head in defeat. "There's no way a shovel could...no, there are no weapons on this planet, no mortal who could defeat the Hydra."

"Well, I'm not exactly mortal, so..."

"You only speak with such certainty because you know not the horrors of the Hydra!"

"Don't worry about it, I've got a shovel."

"Hah?"

I understand not the words of humans, thought Lala's mother.

Alan slashed his shovel through the water, completely ignoring water pressure and forming characters with the trail of his "blade." The bubbles along the shovel trail formed a set of words: "Hydra's Secret."

"Bubble Shovel. It's a technique that uses bubbles to transmit information in the water."

"Whaaaaa?!"

It was highly debatable as to whether the shovel was even related at this point, but that was beside the point. As he had done before in the Lactia Republic, Alan dug up information from the bubbles.

"Aha, I get it now. Once, the Hydra was a mage in the time of the ancient kingdom. He fell in love with a mermaid, but because he was of the land and she of the sea, his love was never fulfilled. However, he refused to give up on her and came upon a forbidden magic that would allow him to become one with the ocean. Unfortunately, this led him to fall to the darkness and he transformed into a horrid monster... I see." Alan narrowed his eyes. "I have all the info I need. He'll be a tough cookie, but I should be able to win."

"Wait, no, what? Um? Huuuuh?!" Lala's mother was beyond perplexed. How could this shovel man know the mermaid legend she hadn't yet even told her daughter?

"Shovelly amazing! What a shovelly sad story..." Lithisia wore a melancholy expression and looked oddly crushed. "In pursuit of love, he tried to become the ocean itself... How very shovel of him..."

Catria had no idea what the princess was talking about, but she could at least tell Lithisia seemed depressed.

Alan nodded. "Anyway, that's about all the information I need. Leave this to me, ma'am."

Lala's mother shook her head. "I-Impossible. Even if you could face the Hydra, we're being held in a prison. There's no way you could defeat the skilled mermen soldiers guarding us."

"How many are there?"

"At least three hundred in the shrine. In total, I'd say about five thousand..."

"Got it. And how many mermaids are being held captive?"

"Huh?" Lala's mother froze up just as her daughter's face lit with hope.

"Alan!" Lala cried, delighted.

"Thirty-two, but...no, please, you must take Lala and flee..."

"All righty then. Just stay where you are."

"Huh?!"

Zoooooooooooom.

Particles of Shovel Power gathered at the tip of Alan's shovel. Saving the captive mermaids would be simple. Rescuing people from underwater prisons was something of the shovel's specialty, after all.

"SCOOP!"

As Alan shouted, splash splash! A mermaid appeared at the head of Alan's shovel. She looked identical to her psychic projection—and to the little mermaid staring at her in bated hope.

"Mommy?!"

"Huh? Eeek...er, Lala?! But how?!"

"Aaaaah! Mommy! Thank goodness! Thank goodness!!!" Lala sobbed as she hugged her mother, who was floating without moving, still in shock.

Catria wasn't much better. *Whoa, c'mon. What the hell is this madness? I mean, I get that shovels are always ridiculous, but this is a step too far. I have no goddamn clue what just happened!*

Even Lithisia was a little flabbergasted until she gasped and clapped her hands together. "I get it! Catria, I totally get it!"

"Please explain what you have supposedly 'gotten.'"

"Shoveling typically consists of 'digging' and 'burying,' no? But when you shovel water..." Lithisia held her shovel in front of her and wiggled it through the current. "The action turns into scooping, right? In other words, you're 'removing' the water! Hence, removing a prisoner!"

Catria felt like everything within her had become solid; air no longer passed through her lungs, and her blood no longer flowed.

"Sir Miner truly is shovelly awesome! I can't even begin to hide all of my shovelwonderment!"

Catria felt her temperature drop. As she continued to sense the slow death of her soul, Alan continued to scoop mermaids out of their prison. Each time he waved his shovel through the water, a mermaid splashed off of its metal head.

"I get it! Since they're mermaids, this is basically like goldfish scooping!"

"It is impossible to follow your chain of 'logic.'"

"You should watch carefully and learn how to use this, Catria. Saving people is part of being a Holy Knight!"

"That may be true...but shovels have nothing to do with it."

"I certainly think they shovelly do!"

Lithisia looked disappointed, but Catria refused to budge on this point. *I'm going to save the world with my blade. Not a shovel!*

"Great, that's everyone."

"You all here!" Lala crowed as she and the other mermaids danced in celebration of their reunion.

Meanwhile, Catria prevented herself from breaking out into a dance of confusion.

"Catria, it's time to conquer the Deep Sea Shrine," said Alan. "Come with me."

"I'm not sure I'm up for this..."

"Weren't you going to become the number one Holy Knight in all the land?"

"Ack!" Catria had no choice but to take this seriously once those words were tossed in her face.

He's right. This shovel man and Shovel Princess are always being shovel-heads, shovelly...crap! What do I mean by shovelly?! I'm being corrupted! I have to hang on to myself. I have to keep my wits as a Holy Knight! I must! That's right. I promised to become a Holy Knight and save the world from the corruption of the shovel! A-and I'm also going to save the mermaids! I'm going to become strong enough to save everyone!

Having managed to get a grip on herself, Catria drew her Holy Knight Blade from her back. "O-of course! Tally ho, Alan!"

"Perfect. First we're going to turn the Deep Sea Shrine into the Land Shrine."

"Hold up."

Alan did not hold up. He pierced the water with his shovel ever so slightly, and suddenly a deep sea volcano erupted...right beneath the shrine. The titanic explosion caused the earth itself to rise above the water, taking the shrine with it.

The mermen did all they could to flee.

"See here, I dug up a deep sea volcano with my shovel."

"Yes, of course, obviously."

In a mere thirty seconds, the Deep Sea Shrine had become the Land Shrine. Alan and the others rose to the surface of the water to watch as the shrine shed sheets of water like a submarine coming up for air.

"..."

Impossible, Catria thought to herself before a chill ran down her spine. An eldritch malice emanated from the shrine. Something awful lurked within. Its monstrous presence was exactly the same as the Red Dragon's in the desert nation.

"How dare you... How dare you take my precious mermaids!" A tidal wave of rage rushed out of the shrine and transformed into pure, overwhelming menace.

"... (Shoveling shoveltache...)"

Lithisia appeared to be thinking something as she set her gaze upon it. As for what that something was, there was little doubt that it was probably a shovel.

"You will pay!!!" the thunder roared.

The entire shrine shone a vivid poison green, and in the next moment, it transformed into a monster with multiple tentacles, not unlike an octopus. A glowing green aura surrounded every part of its body, and a noxious ooze dripped from its dangerous mouth. It was a horrible sight to behold.

This was the sea monster Hydra? No wonder the mermaids were so terrified.

However, Catria kept her cool. The Lernia Hydra was a dreadful sight and its aura was terrifying. However... "It's certainly no shovel... Whoa, hold it!"

What am I thinking?! Has my thought process been corrupted?!

Leaving Catria to her panic, Alan made his move. When he flew into the sky, he collected the light of blue Shovel Power into the head of his shovel. The energy was summoned from the ocean, the mermaids, Lithisia, and even the Ultimate Shovel where it drifted nearby.

Power charge: 120 percent. Target: locked on.

"Wave Motion Shovel Blast, DIG!"

"OOOOUUUH?!"

KA-CHOOOOOOOOM!

Alan shot off a profound mass of energy from his shovel, one many times larger than the Hydra's body. It tore into the ocean, cutting right through the temple and piercing both heaven and earth. Hundreds of giant tentacles were evaporated in the beam of light.

Welp. No mercy, as always.

Once the light vanished, all that remained was a handful of giant tentacles.

"Alan...Alan, amazing! Humans, amazing!" Lala called.

"Lala, it's times like this that you should be cheering, 'Hip, hip, shovelay! Hip, hip, shovelay!'"

"Huh? Oh, okay! Hip, hip shovelay! Hip, hip, shovelay!"

Lithisia was extremely satisfied.

The mermaids watched on in silence as the remains of the Hydra sunk beneath the ocean. Catria let out a tiny sigh. How anticlimactic it all was. A creature said to be a god of the sea stood no chance against the mighty shovel.

What the hell are shovels? Catria thought to herself.

SWISH!

"I'm...taking you...with me..."

One of the remaining tentacles thrashed. Its tip headed straight toward Lala at delirious speed. This was the Hydra's vicious final attack, its dying blitz.

"?!"

Crap! Lala's going to get hit! thought Catria. *Alan hasn't noticed the tentacle yet—I have to save her.*

Catria swung her "Holy Knight Blade." The tentacle was too far away. Her blade would never reach it. Nonetheless, Catria somehow felt like she could hit it. She could feel herself collecting holy energy from within herself and the Ultimate Shovel into the head of her Holy Knight Blade.

"Lala!" shouted Catria.

"Eeek!"

Without thinking of anything other than "scooping" Lala away from her current predicament...Catria swung her Holy Knight Blade toward the tentacle she couldn't hope to reach.

In that instant, the head of her sword expanded to form a shovel.

"OOOOOHHH!!!" Catria cried out to the sky, almost as if she were being controlled by some greater power. "SAVE!"

SHIZOOOOOMBAAAAMM!!!!

She fired a beam.

"..."

The beam of energy ripped the tentacle in twain and its separate parts dropped into the ocean.

Catria came to after hearing the noise. "Er, uh, wha?"

In a daze, she stared at the tip of her sword. Something had definitely come out of it. A beam. It had been far thinner than Alan's Wave Motion Shovel Blast, but she was certain she had fired off a beam of concentrated holy energy in the shape of a cross.

It might as well have been pure instinct. As if it were the most natural thing in the world, she shot a beam just by desiring to save Lala and believing she could.

"Thank you! Thank you, Catria!"

"Er, uh, um... W-wait just a second Lala. I..."

"Catria! You're amazing! You really did a shovel!" Lithisia was so moved she was shaking her shovel. Her smile was radiant with joy at seeing one of her very own had awakened to the art of the shovel.

As she processed what had just happened, fear struck deep within Catria. *Did I really just shovel?*

"No, you're wrong! Alan! You did something, didn't you?!"

"Not a thing." Alan landed on the ground and smirked at Catria. "Not bad at all. It may have been the basic terrain form, but you definitely just fired off a Wave Motion Shovel Blast."

"I knew it! Catria, your Wave Motion Shovel Blast was just the most shovelingly beautiful!" Lithisia hopped up and down in excitement, her eyes glistening.

In contrast, Catria looked like she had seen a ghost. *No, this can't be. That's impossible!*

Alan continued to analyze her attack. "Your desire to 'save' as a Holy Knight and the concept of 'scooping' with a shovel came together."

"No, no, no, no!"

"Whatever do you shovelly mean?"

"I just...that wasn't a Wave Motion Shovel Blast!" Catria thought for a moment before yelling out to the heavens. "That was a Wave Motion Sword! A sword technique called, uh, the 'Justice Stream'!"

"Jushovelream?"

"No! Justice! Even the incantation is 'save'!"

"Isn't it all the same, shovel?"

The three continued to go at it. Meanwhile, Lala and the other mermaids swam up to them. They expressed their gratitude one by one for saving both their people and Lala.

"Catria, you like Alan. Amazing! Shovelly amazing!"

"Stop it, Lala. Please! That wasn't a shovel!" Catria's cries disappeared over the horizon.

"Now then, everyone! Let's have a Shovel Party tonight!"

And so the crew enjoyed a banquet of sorts at the Mermaid Oasis until late in the evening. The joyful Lala, the tear-filled rampaging Catria, and Alice, who was still asleep. The banquet continued deep into the night.

That was how Alan and Catria became a part of mermaid legend.

Unfortunately, everyone had completely forgotten about the Green Orb. It wouldn't be until the party returned to Lactia that Catria would come to her senses on this very subject after they had already checked in to the inn.

Alice's Warm Body Shovel

LET'S REWIND A BIT. It was late at night, and a completely nude young woman was standing on the deck of the Ultimate Shovel as it sailed back to the Lactia Republic.

"Haaah... Finally, some peace and quiet."

Alice had come out for a walk beneath the stars and was meandering across the deck of the Ultimate Shovel. This was her chance to retrieve peace of mind after being forced to participate in the mermaid scoop dance at the banquet.

Despite appearances, Alice was an undead king, and she therefore didn't need sleep (though she sometimes liked it). That was why she was able to go for walks when the humans, or to be more specific, the Shovel Princess, was asleep. This was her self-care, and it prevented her from being completely corrupted by the dreaded shovel.

"The night belongs to me... Heh, I guess not."

Alice looked toward the mast, where atop the crow's nest were two men of the sea. Alice emitted a faint light, so she stood out against the darkness and the watchmen soon took notice of her.

"Vice Captain Alice! Thank you for doing the Shovel Rounds!"

Lithisia's corruption had long since spread throughout the ship.

"Ha ha, fear not! We're keeping careful watch on the seas!"

As Alice stood silent without showing any sign of response, the watchman came down to report what he'd seen. He produced a metal tube resembling a long-range scope, except the hole at the end wasn't in the shape of a circle; it was a triangle.

"This here be 'Shovelscope', equipped with a Shovel Lens. With this contraption, I can see all the way beyond the horizon!"

Indeed, Lithisia's corruption was everywhere (despairingly so.)

"By applying a lens to the surface of a shovel, you can see farther than with an ordinary convex lens! It's crazy!"

"Are you trying to pick a fight with the laws of physics?" asked Alice.

"No, really! You can see things you otherwise couldn't! Take a look!"

Alice grabbed the Shovelscope and stuck it to her face. Indeed, the triangular lens displayed an array of video images side by side, little windows into different locations. In one, the Lactia Republic's shovel-shaped flag snapped in the wind; in another, mermaids frolicked in their oasis; in an image in the corner, Alice saw into the captain's quarters.

"Apparently, the lens allows you to see anything with a 'shovel' attribute," said the watchman.

"I don't think you can get away with describing this as a lens."

As Alice perused the Shovelscope's images, one of the windows began to display a new feed. It showed a white princess dress and long blonde hair, both of which belonged to Lithisia. Well, *she* certainly qualified as having a shovel attribute. Presently, she was walking along one of the passages within the ship, and she appeared to be headed for the deck.

Alice had an epiphany. "If I use this contraption, I could always stay one step ahead of her, no?"

The Shovelscope revealed anything related to shovels. If she got her hands on it, she'd know Lithisia's location at all times. No matter where Alice hid, Lithisia always found her with her own bizarre Shovel Senses. But with this scope, Alice might at last escape her grasp.

"Hee hee hee..." Alice grinned as she watched Lithisia approach.

Suddenly, the princess turned around. "Oh, my. If it isn't Alice!"

SCOOOOP (the sound Lithisia made when she smiled)!

Lithisia was looking directly into Alice's eyes through the Shovelscope.

"EEEEEEEEEEK!!!"

It was a truly horrific experience. Alice had stared deep into the abyss of the shovel, and it had stared right on back.

"Y-you want to discuss something?"

Thirty seconds later, Alice found herself in the captain's quarters. According to the princess, Alice had been sucked through the lens of the Shovelscope and transported to Lithisia's location by a process called "Shovel Warping." Alice could tell she was in danger and Alice-juices trickled from her skin, but Lithisia smiled.

"Yes! Would you hear me out, shovel?" Lithisia asked, holding her glistening red shovel with a smile.

Alice could do nothing but nod as quickly as nonhumanly possible. "So, um, what's on your mind?"

Do you actually even worry about things?! Alice wanted to add, but in the face of extreme peril, she held her tongue.

In turn, Lithisia nodded, oddly meek. "I'm thinking about the future."

"The future?"

"As you're well aware, I want to become a shovel."

This was already an impossible desire, but Alice had no choice but to keep listening. That said, the princess's next words proved to be a surprise.

"Have I lost my way...?"

"Excuse me...?" Alice stared. *She's seriously asking me this now?*

At Alice's complete silence, Lithisia continued. "To be honest, I didn't really grasp what 'becoming a shovel' truly meant."

"I don't think any human does."

"But over the last few days, I think I've come to understand, just a little."

"And why's that?"

"After learning all about that sea monster, the Hydra..."

Lithisia was troubled by the tragic tale of the Hydra Alan had uncovered. The creature came to be due to a man's love for a mermaid and his desire to become the "ocean" itself. His tragic end...could that be what awaited Lithisia at the end of her journey to become a shovel for the man she loved? After all, the ocean and the shovel were so very similar in the way they were so very great and majestic.

"..."

They're not even remotely alike. Meh, but I suppose I can understand where she's coming from, Alice thought, though she refused to accept that the two things were at all similar.

Lithisia clutched her red shovel close to her chest, her uncertainty plainly visible. "Am I fated to one day become a monster like the Hydra?"

Arguably, you've already become one. Alice truly believed that. She was about to say as much but stopped herself. Lithisia really seemed to be concerned about all of this. *Now that I think about it, this could be the chance of a lifetime.*

If Alice could correct Lithisia's Shovel Course, even just a little bit... This opportunity wouldn't come again anytime soon.

"If that's the case..." Alice bowed her head in thought. "You must seek the warmth of others."

"Warmth?" Lithisia tilted her head.

"Precisely. Before I met you and Alan, I was but a cold-blooded monster. I only ever communed with creatures like myself. The undead who served me, the demon Zeleburg... I'm certain the Hydra was the same." Alice recalled with cold clarity her dark days as a creature of the night. Had she not met Lithisia and Alan, she most certainly would've destroyed the part of herself that was "Alice." As conflicted as she was about the whole shoveling situation, that much was undoubtedly true. "I personally believe humans become monsters when they lose touch with the warmth of others."

"Become monsters..."

"That's why, Lithisia, I have a suggestion." Alice pointed her finger to the heavens, and like a priestess of prophecy, she made her declaration. "You must seek the warmth of another! The lady knight. The girl of nobility. The elf and the sage. Fortunately, you are surrounded by many friends and allies. If you take great care of your bonds with these individuals and work to solidify them, you will never become a monster like I did."

Lithisia's eyes were locked on Alice. "Warmth... I see."

Deep within, Alice cackled as she watched the princess nod. *I did it! I'm the best! Now my pain and suffering will be no more!*

Hypothesis: Lithisia interacts more with flesh-and-blood humans.

Consequently: Her time to interact with Alice decreases.

Conclusion: Alice will be shoveled less!

It was the perfect formula. Alice could at last disperse some of her Shovel Suffering (hundreds of times worse than the salt air). This was wonderful. Ever since their visit to the Lactia Republic, Alice had been shoveled daily, and even Alice had to admit she'd started to somewhat enjoy the sensation. This in and of itself told her she was headed down a terribly dangerous path.

I did it!

But just as Alice began to celebrate...out of nowhere, Lithisia enveloped Alice in a soft embrace.

"Yah!"

"Eek!" The undead king looked up to find Lithisia smiling down at her. "What are you... Hey, I'm cold-blooded! You're not going to get any warmth outta me."

"Oh, that's fine. I'm not using you to warm up. It's the shovessite (opposite)."

"Wha?"

"I thought maybe I might warm you up instead." Lithisia giggled as she held Alice even more tightly. "If I ever became a shovel, a being beyond that of a human...I doubt there'd be any humans who'd want to be around me. That's why I need to make sure you don't ever go back to being a monster, Alice. I have to keep you nice and warm and by my side."

"I-I was talking about *you* before, not me...!"

"*I'll* stay nice and warm just by standing near Sir Miner."

Lithisia pressed Alice's face into her bountiful breasts. She smelled delightful, and even though Alice didn't need to breathe air, she couldn't stop taking in the princess-fragrance. This was crazy. Totally crazy. She was going to become addicted to this aroma.

Things would turn out poorly if she didn't stop now. Alice knew what came next.

"W-wait, stop! Please, no shoveling!!!" said Alice. If Lithisia shoveled her while she was in her current condition... It'd be over. The end. Kaputsies. She couldn't allow that to happen. "If you take out a shovel now, I'll pass on to the next life! I swear it!"

Lithisia nodded at the odd threat. "That's too bad... Then I suppose I'll just have to settle with rubby shoveling you with my hands."

"Y-you better keep your promise!"

Just as Lithisia said she would, she slowly ran her hands across Alice's back. Nice...and slow...

ZIIING!

"!!!"

Alice stretched her arms and legs out, her mouth open

and expression strained. It took only a single moment for Alice to reach her limit.

"How?! You're just using your hands!"

"Didn't I tell you? I've come to understand a little about what 'becoming a shovel' means."

"Hah?!"

"I realized something. When you do this with a human hand..." Lithisia brought her long white fingers in front of Alice and stretched them out. She then stroked them across the middle of Alice's back. With her middle finger as the apex of her hand, it resembled a thin triangle of sorts. Her hand shone in the faint light of the ship. "It's just like a shovel."

SO WHAT?! Alice cried out in her heart.

It was too late for Lithisia. She had unconsciously long since given up on being a human. "And so it's time to get you nice and shovely warm. Get ready!"

"Shovely warm?!"

Lithisia rested the surface of her hand on Alice's thighs. Then she began to rubba dub dub!

"Gaahhhh!!!"

And so Alice began to shovely dovely all the rubba dub dubbly.

Shuffle, shuffle, swish swish.

Alice could do nothing to resist.

"I can feel your warmth..." Lithisia cooed. "Ah, this is truly the correct form of the shovel!"

You're wrong! thought Alice, but she had neither the strength nor energy to say as much.

On this day, Lithisia took more steps forward as a Shovel Princess.

PART 30
Li'l Fio's Welcome Home Shovel

AFTER GOING BACK to the Mermaid Oasis to retrieve the Green Orb and saying their goodbyes to Lucrezia, the crew left the Lactia Republic. They made their way home to the World Tree Castle, where Fio the elf girl met them warmly at the towering gates. She had seen them from the third-floor balcony, and with a bright expression she rushed down to meet them, her breasts swaying.

"Welcome home, Uncle Alan!" Fio spread her arms wide and smiled as dazzlingly as the sun itself.

In return, Alan smoothed the palm of his hand over her head. "Thanks. Glad to see you're doing well, Fio."

"I'm just...so glad you're all o...kay?" Fio glanced at the horse and carriage behind Alan. Sitting in the back were the lady knight and the naked undead girl, completely petrified.

"Um, Catria and Alice look like they've seen ghosts."

"Yeah, well..." Alan rubbed the back of his neck. "Catria's exhausted because I used my new Shovel Home Run to fly us home from the Lactia Republic, I guess."

"Shovel...Home Run?"

"It's a technique where I use a shovel to hit the carriage a super long distance."

He had developed this technique after studying the popular Lactia Republic sport of "baseball." By scooping his shovel upward, he could imitate an upper swing, allowing him to send a target flying a long distance. Alan's explanation did little to clear things up for Fio.

Er, if he hit the carriage that hard, wouldn't he destroy it? Um, um! But if Lady Lithisia and the carriage are both okay, I guess I shouldn't overthink it!

"What about Alice?" Fio asked.

"Hee, hee..." Alice slumped out of her seat and out of sight. "I...love shovels..."

"O-oh." Fio, clever as she was, could tell she shouldn't dig any further. "I'm not sure I really understand, but I do know you're amazing, Uncle Alan!"

Fio was an elf girl as open-minded as she was large-breasted.

"Fio... Are you really...okay with that?" Catria muttered.

70

"This carriage has definitely been shovelfied..." Alice groaned.

Catria and Alice both attempted to speak, but came off more like zombies moaning into the wind.

At that point, Lithisia merrily disembarked from the carriage. "Sir Miner, I suggest we take a break inside and perhaps shovey wovey for a bit."

"A break sounds good," he agreed. "But no shovey woveying."

"No? Aww..."

Fio leaned in curiously. "Lady Lithisia, what exactly is shovey woveying?"

Lithisia's eyes sparkled as she drew close to Fio's ear and whispered the answer.

As she murmured, Fio's cheeks turned utterly pink and her eyes darted about. She held her hands to her chest, inadvertently accentuating her breasts. "O-oh my gosh! That's what it means?!"

"Hee hee, indeed, shovel."

"G-gosh, oh gosh..."

Alan hastily pulled the two of them apart. "Stop poisoning Fio's mind with your shovel education nonsense."

"My apologies, but I just thought even elves needed a little shovey wovey goodness."

"I'm not even going to pretend I follow, but I think you're the only one who needs that."

"Eh? Er, um, ah..." Lithisia happily put her fingers together as she squirmed about. "I-I am a Shovel Princess, a-after all."

Perhaps it would've been better for all parties involved if they had left this princess in the Lactia Republic.

After sharing tales of their adventures with Fio, Alan and the others decided to take a whole day to rest. Alan notwithstanding, Catria and Alice were clearly wiped, and the group also needed to review the new information they'd acquired.

Around evening, Alan whipped up a marble bathhouse and was having a soak to test it out. It was about as large as a small throne room and could fit approximately one hundred people. This sort of structure would be a municipal necessity for when the elves came back to power.

"I really have to make some time to think that over, too," Alan said to himself, lying back in the steam.

For now, Alan was using his time in the bath to think long and hard about the five orbs in their possession, and what that meant for their journey. In other words, it was almost over.

Once this quest was finished, Alan would return to his mountain, but before that, he had to fulfill his promise to Fio: the promise to help restore the elves to their former glory. For the time being, he had crafted the World Tree Castle, a means to keep the elves safe. But that wasn't enough to revive an entire civilization. For that, one needed not only people, but an economy, culture, and all sorts of other things.

It would be impossible for someone as young as Fio to do all by herself. Alan had to consider what was possible for him to contribute...and what he should leave to her.

Just then, Alan heard the quiet shift of water as someone else entered the bath. *Well, it's a fairly huge bathhouse, so that's no big deal...*

"No, wait a sec."

Was he not currently the only man in the elf castle?

The splashing drew closer and closer. Soon, Alan could make out the silhouette of a pointy-eared individual hidden within the steam. Next, he identified their skin color. Then, their considerable...assets. Their tips were concealed by sheer clouds of heat.

It was Fio.

It appeared as though she knew someone else was present, but couldn't make out his face. She approached with a blithe smile. "Um, it's me, Fio. Lithisia? Catria?"

"Ah, no," said Alan. "It's me..."

"Huh?" Fio froze. Only her breasts maintained their softness, bouncing up and down due to the abruptness with which she stopped in her tracks. She was submerged in the water from the waist down, so Alan couldn't see anything below the water line, but depending on one's perspective, this meant he could see everything else.

Fio the elf girl was more or less nude in front of him.

Her cheeks turned crimson. "Er, um, Uncle...Alan...I... EEEEEEK!"

In one fell swoop, Fio plopped her entire body underneath the water and balled up in embarrassment. Unfortunately, this left her back and nape totally defenseless, charming in their own right.

Alan groaned. "I thought I told Lithisia it'd be 'men's only' for a while."

"All she told me was it was going to be 'shovels only,' so no shovely doveling!"

"Ugh, I'm so sorry, this is all my fault." Alan was an idiot for trusting the dastardly princess with any sort of message. "Look, I'll get out."

"Eh? No, wait! I-I'm the one who intruded on your bath!"

"Fio, um, if you move like that...I can—"

"EEEEK!"

Back down she went.

This time, Fio dove so deeply into the water that even her mouth was submerged. Even then, the shadow of her breasts swaying beneath the surface were all too distinct. Alan averted his eyes, but realized it was impossible to avoid her completely. In his long days as a miner, he had acquired the Shovel Eye, an ability that made him wary to every little detail in even the darkest of surroundings. As such, he was unable to stop picking up on every one of Fio's little movements. In the dim, her skin shivered.

"Ah, you…really notice everything, huh…?" Fio said as she contorted her body, trying to better cover herself.

This was bad. The longer Alan stayed, the worse he felt. Time to get the heck out. Alan started to rise from the bath.

"N-no, please wait!" Fio pleaded. It appeared as though she'd come to some sort of inner conclusion. "Um, I, um…it's fine…it's fine if you can see me…!"

"It absolutely isn't! You're a young, unmarried woman. How could any of this be fine?"

"It's…embarrassing, but…" Fio hid her mouth with her hand and continued faintly. "I'm going to show you everything when we shovel together…so…"

"Er, come again?"

What was this buxom elf girl going on about? Sure, Alan had promised to "shovel" with her, by which he meant he was going to craft a hero's statue for the home of the elves. What did her body, nude or otherwise, have to do with sculpting?

Wait a minute.

Hrmph, in other words...

Alan nodded, newly confident. "So you're saying you want me to carve you (a statue)."

"Augh... E-er, I mean, more specifically, 'dig' me!" Fio flailed and covered her face with her hands.

Why was she being so shy? "Hm, but does it really need to be you (as a model)?"

"Huh?" Fio looked puzzled.

"I've seen many great elven heroes and heroines in my time."

"Er, um, I, but they're all dead."

"Even if they are, I can still carve them (in a sculpting fashion)."

"You can (in a child-making fashion)?!" Fio was the most startled she'd been all day. Her breasts rocked, almost emerging from the water. Fio was too surprised to notice. "Ah, b-but I suppose Alice is undead, so I guess that makes sense?!"

"I mean, it's certainly easier to do the deed with some-one still alive (in a modeling sense), but as long as I can remember what they looked like, it's fine."

"It's fine?!"

"Heck, Pasarunak often did it with dead elves."

"He did?!" Fio's mental image of Pasarunak grew grim and distant.

"Oh, wait! What if I did Pasarunak? He was one of the grandest elves of all."

"Lord Pasarunak...? No, no, no! He's a man!"

"What does that have to do with anything? Pasarunak paid no mind to those sorts of things."

"He didn't?!" Fio's mental image of Pasarunak became even more distant and obscure.

The pair had yet to notice a fearsome misunderstand-ing was still underway.

"Haaah, haaah, I'm so shocked..." Fio murmured.

"That's why it doesn't necessarily have to be you," Alan explained, feeling proud of himself for solving Fio's prob-lems. "Especially since you're so flustered."

As far as Alan could tell, what Fio desired was a statue of a nude woman. In other words, she thought she herself would have to undress and model for him. But between her age and their status as adopted family, Alan consid-ered this a dubious proposition at best.

"U-um..." Fio poked her index fingers together. "I-It's certainly flustering, but...I, um... I know I'm not suitable as a partner, but...even then!"

Even then, Fio thought as she bit her lip.

"I still want you to shovel me, Uncle Alan..." She ker-plunked into the water again. "You saved me, Uncle Alan. Y-you've been so kind to me...and no matter how much we talk, I just feel so at ease and safe. Th-that's why, um, it's hard to put into words, but!"

"No... That's more than enough. I understand." Alan clenched his fist with determination. "I'll do it."

Honestly, at this rate, he'd agree to anything to avoid subjecting the girl to more indignity. Alan decided to sculpt Fio with all her elegance and all his might.

Fio smiled, relieved by this turn of events. She stood and expressed her gratitude over and over again. "Thank you so much! Thank you oh so much!"

Tragically, her bouncing breasts now occupied the majority of Alan's line of sight.

Oh boy... he thought, averting his Shovel Eyes as best he could. Fio truly was a remarkable specimen. If Alan made a statue modeled after her, it might invite all manner of concerning male tourists.

"Ah, eeek!" As soon as Fio noticed Alan's strained expression, she hastily covered her breasts, etc. "Ah, I-I'm sorry. I know you'll need to see things properly in order to do your work..."

"No, no. The form of someone covering themselves is—*artistic*. It's perfect for shoveling. Keep up the good work."

"It is...? Um, er, so..." Fio pressed her arms deep into the valley of her chest. She hesitated for a moment, then spoke again. "Do you think, um, I'm...shovelly enough...?"

It took a full five seconds for Alan to understand what was happening. Well, not quite. It took five seconds for Alan to understand that he had no flipping clue what was going on. "My apologies, but could you translate that into regular words?"

"Oh, um, I'm sorry... Apparently 'shovelly' is an adjective that refers to something that makes you instinctively want to shovel. It was listed in Rostir's basic dictionary."

"Burn that dictionary."

The future of Rostir's educational system was in dire straits.

"Hm, but I suppose in that sense, yes, you are sufficiently 'shovelly,'" said Alan.

"R-really?!"

"I've seen all manner of elves in my lifetime, but you are undoubtedly the most 'shovelly' of them all."

Within this pure elf was a contradictory innate allure. She would make for a splendid statue, even if it would be primarily for men.

Fio's cheeks turned pink and tears welled in her eyes. Her ample breasts swelled. "I...I'm such a happy little shovel... Ah!"

Perhaps due to spending too much time in the bath, Fio lost her balance. Alan panicked and rushed to catch her. Fio fell face-first into Alan's chest, causing her chest to make contact with his. She was wondrously soft to say the least, like some kind of softness that existed just to be tenderly touched and touch in turn.

"Ah...ah!"

Beneath Fio's delicate shoulders was a spectacular figure. With heavy eyes, Fio leaned her entire body up against Alan.

Alan was suddenly compelled to make her feel safe. "Fio, next time I come back, let's shovel as much as we can."

"As much as we can?!"

"I'll put my everything into it. I'll make a hundred of 'em for you."

"O-one hundred?! Oh gosh!" Fio's eyes spiraled out of control as her golden locks waved in the water.

And so another night passed in the World Tree Castle. The misunderstanding between the elf and the miner was speeding in the direction of the almighty shovel, thanks to a home run shot.

The following day, the party assembled in the great hall to hold a roundtable meeting. Before they could search out the next orb, they had to review some vital new information.

"Apparently, we've received a Vision Orb from Prime Minister Zeleburg," said Alan.

"Hmph. Has he figured out we're using the World Tree Castle as our base of operations?" Catria asked.

Alan shook his head. "No. The orb was delivered to an inn in Shilasia, the ice nation."

"Huh? Why?"

"According to Zeleburg's intelligence, we're currently 'on our way home from Shilasia.'"

"Let me guess, you buried the truth again, right?"

In any event, they played the Vision Orb. An image unfurled from within it, and they were greeted with the sight of Zeleburg's beautiful human form clad in a majestic cape.

"Greetings, my dear Princess Lithisia. Let me congratulate you on acquiring two orbs."

"That number doesn't add up, Alan," said Catria. "Don't we have more?"

"Don't worry, I buried the truth about that too. In addition to the one Lithisia already had, he thinks we only acquired the Silver Orb from Shilasia."

"However, I must warn you," Zeleburg continued. "The remaining orbs reside with my most powerful of underlings, the Tetrad Archfiends. The 'Red Dragon of the Desert,' the 'Undead King,' the 'Archfiend of the Great Sea.' The strength of any one of these great monsters rivals that of the gods themselves. They look upon mankind as naught but garbage!"

"Ouch..." Catria couldn't help pitying the prime minister. All these monsters had been instantly eliminated by Alan's Wave Motion Shovel Blast. The Undead King Alice was present and accounted for, but she was a victim of the shovel in her own way.

"And then there's the most powerful of the Tetrad Archfiends, the 'Emperor of the Sky', Pazuzu! Even I am incapable of controlling him fully. He is very nearly a god of destruction. And as his name implies, he resides in the great sky, the floating city of Rahzelfo. Yes, the very same one from the legends of the ancient magic kingdom! Humans cannot fly, my dear Princess Lithisia." Zeleburg scoffed. "However, I'm willing to offer you a chance.

There is a magic teleportation ring that will take you to Rahzelfo located to the southwest of Rostir on an island deep within the Remote Ruins. Fear not, Princess. I will welcome you with open arms. I'll be waiting."

Zeleburg smiled just before the video cut off.

Catria was beginning to worry that he was perhaps the most unfortunate demon in the entire world.

"Sir Miner, looks like we have our next destination!" Lithisia declared.

"Indeed. We're journeying to the floating city. In other words..."

Alan hoisted his shovel with a clank and a light blue aura shimmered around it. Then the aura shot from his shovel and arced toward the carriage in the garden. On contact, the entire vehicle bobbed gently into the air.

"It's shoveling time."

How long will Zeleburg wait for Lithisia at these so-called Remote Ruins before he realizes she's never going to show? Catria thought to herself. As Catria imagined that scenario, she found herself slightly at ease. *Finally, I've found someone worse off than I am.*

Shovel Suit
Equipment: Full Body Armor

RARITY
SSR (Scoopy Shovel Rare)

EXPLANATION
A piece of equipment imbued with magical (Shovel) Power. The High Priestess of the Holy Shovel Faith created this for her Shovel Friend. While at first glance it appears to be a pure white, silk leotard with silver decorations, on the inside are 4,545 hyper-fine shovel heads in constant contact with the skin. The friction created by the movement of these hyper-fine shovel heads continuously provides extreme pleasure to the wearer for all eternity.

EQUIPMENT EFFECTS
- Attack +45
- Defense +45
- Shovel Power +4545

SPECIAL EFFECTS
① Shovel Suit Trap:
The moment this suit is equipped, the wearer falls under the effects of "Shovel Arousal." When under the effects of "Shovel Arousal," the mind suffers from shovel corruption, and all actions unrelated to shovels have a four out of five chance of being canceled.

② All Hail the Shovel Princess:
The wearer cannot disobey the High Priestess of the Holy Shovel Faith. They must do or shovel whatever she asks of them.

③ They're Not Tentacles So They're Totes Fine:
They're not tentacles, they're shovels.

HOLY SHOVEL EMPIRE, OFFICIAL DICTIONARY
(AUTHOR: LITHISIA), 21ST VERSION.

CHAPTER 7

The Sky Nation's Shovel

(LUCY'S INTO IT)

PART 31

The Princess (Attempts to) Shovel an Angel

O N THE ROOF of the World Tree Castle, Catria gazed up at the blue sky.

The legendary floating city of Rahzelfo, huh?

At its most prosperous, the ancient kingdom of magic built Rahzelfo using the most advanced magical technologies and crystals at their disposal. Rahzelfo's architects dreamed of a paradise where the masters of various schools of magics could live and learn in peace. A land of the gods, so to speak.

However, when those who had been excluded from the floating city revolted against the magic kingdom, they burned everything in sight to the ground using magic weapons known as "Heaven's Flames." These terrible fires even changed the shape of the continent.

All of this was, of course, the stuff of ancient myth and legend. But according to Zeleburg, Rahzelfo really did exist, and it was still floating above the clouds...and they were headed there to search for the Golden Orb.

This was the kind of adventure every Holy Knight dreamed of!

"Now then, everyone get on the carriage," said Alan. "I'm going to send it flying with a Shovel Home Run."

"Please don't!" Catria moaned, desperately trying to protect her dreams of swashbuckling adventure.

Meanwhile, Alan prepared to make the hit with his shovel. He let his foot wave a bit, taking a kannushi batting stance. He was a power hitter with a home run average of 1.0. The only disadvantage was he could only play as an SDH (an offshoot of a designated hitter (DH), utilized by the Shovel League). With a single hit, he could send a straight ball flying like an intercontinental shovel missile.

"Hah?!" Catria shook off whatever weird vision had taken over her. Her mind was already off the rails, and she had to do what she could to cling to sweet, sweet common sense. "W-wait, Alan! Don't ruin the moment!"

"Catria, stop trying to run away from reality, shovel."

"Just give up. I have," Alice sniffed.

"I will not bend the knee! And how are we even going to get home?! Are we going to just fall?!"

"Ah, yeah, good point." Alan fell out of his stance.

"I know! We have to do this the proper way!" In other words, Catria wanted them to use the teleportation magic in the Remote Ruins.

"Then how about this," said Alan. "I'll build stairs."

"Stairs?"

Shoof, shoof, shoof, stairs!

"Perfect. There you go."

A mere thirty seconds later, Alan had completed a set of stairs stretching from the roof of the World Tree Castle all the way to the end of the sky. It was approximately ten feet wide and seemingly went on for ages.

Miners were great at making stairs; Alan had once built stairs straight to Hell—6,666,666 steps total—so he could more efficiently carry out precious stones. This time around, he built ten million steps.

"Not bad, if I do say so myself."

He had used transparent mythril silver for this particular stairway. As such, it was effectively invisible from a distance. Zeleburg would have no idea the stairs even existed.

"My word, Sir Miner! Now anyone can go from the World Tree Castle to Rahzelfo and back again!"

"You really expect 'anyone' to be able to climb ten million steps?" Alice asked.

"Don't worry, Alice," Alan assured her. "I've installed a rest area at every ten thousand steps so you can get your proper hydration."

And if somebody were to get injured, these rest areas were each equipped with a first aid box and even a parachute, just in case. Of course, there were also beds. For miners, safety was paramount.

"You're shovelly amazing, Sir Miner! Are there also places to replenish our shovelness?"

"I'm pretty sure you can do that naturally all on your own, Lithisia."

"W-wow, really?" For some reason, Lithisia responded bashfully.

Catria gazed at the set of stairs before her. Their ethereal translucence stretched to the end of the sky. It was like a staircase to heaven.

No, it wasn't *like*, it actually *was*.

It's finally my time to go on an adventure as a Holy Knight!

And just like that, Catria tricked herself into being excited about the upcoming escapade. She pointed to the sun and, with a refreshed smile on her face, shouted. "Let us take to the skies, Alan, Alice, Your Highness! HA HA HA HA!"

Her tone was largely desperate.

"Catria's so sad to watch that it's making me feel bad," Alice said.

"I'm sure it'll be fine, shovel! Shall I shovel you?"

"NOOO! STAY AWAY!"

"C'mon, folks. We're climbing these stairs."

The last chunk of stairs connected to the edge of a vast floating land, in the center of which the party found Rahzelfo, the illustrious city of myth, carved straight from the skybound earth.

"Amazing..." said Catria, despite herself. "The legendary floating city really does exist."

The nearer they drew to the city walls, the more intense the sheer presence of the ancient city became. It was approximately one hundred times larger than the World Tree Castle, but it was also kind of a mess. Ivy grew dense and impenetrable over the crenellations and battlements at the lower tiers.

"It's a shame Alice passed on before she could see this..." Lithisia murmured.

Alice hadn't actually 'passed on,' but she was currently not meaningfully present. She was an unfortunate sacrifice, let's say. More specifically, at one of the rest stops, the princess had used the undead girl to replenish her "shovelness."

"Haaah, that was delicious," said Lithisia at the recollection.

"No, no more... No more shovels..." Catria mumbled. Just remembering what she had witnessed had Catria on the edge of madness, so she retreated with all haste.

Anyhow, the party had finally arrived at Rahzelfo. The ruins of an ancient magical civilization of days long past lay before them. Enormous human-shaped statues and fantastical, if overgrown, buildings stood in magnificent decay. If any court mage were to lay eyes upon this wonder of history, their eyes would shine with abject delight. However, the team's objective right now was the Golden Orb.

"Alan, do you know where the orb is?" asked Catria.

"According to my Shovel Search, it's in the center of this city."

In fact, a large tower as tall as a mountain stood in that very location.

I see, that should've been obvious, thought Catria. *Psh, I'm not gonna let myself get impressed by the likes of a Shovel Search or whatever.*

At that moment, a shining golden brilliance descended from the skies.

"What the...? Are those...wings?" Catria instinctively looked up and swallowed her breath. *Is that an angel...?*

"FEAR THE JUDGMENT OF THE HEAVEEEENS!"

A beautiful, holy voice rang in the party's ears. The origin was the angel floating before them, her pink hair flowing in the wind.

She looked to be about the same age as Catria, but luminous wings sprouted from her back. A halo floated above her head and she wore a gauzy white dress. The party was looking up at her from below, but the censorworthy area beneath her skirt was thoroughly obscured by the light of the sun.

The angel flared with a holy aura as her shining hair drifted about her like a halo. Before her were three monsters with black wings. They wore vicious smiles as they said some tremendously troubling things.

"Female angel! Kill! Kill, violate, bury!"

"Order wrong! Violate *then* bury *then* kill!"

"No way! I like this order!"

"I'm gonna kill and bury YOU!"

"Of what horrors do you speak?! Take thiiiis!"

The angel's sword collided with a demon's claws. They appeared to be about equal in strength, but in light of numbers, the angel was at a disadvantage.

"Alan! Is that a real angel?!" demanded Catria.

A messenger of the gods in Heaven. A being of fairy tales and legends. One who was fighting before Catria's own two eyes.

"A Rank 8 Angel Knight, eh? It's rare for them to be alone. Did they get separated from their allies?"

"You SHKNOW about them?! (You know about them, shovel?!)" gasped Lithisia.

"Oh yeah, sure. I've seen my fair share of angels who had been captured by Hell, tortured, and become fallen."

Lest you forget, this crazy guy had actually mined for stuff in Hell.

But that wasn't important.

Just then, the angel's sword was deflected. Her clothes were being torn to pieces, and her divine bosom was on the verge of being revealed to all.

This is bad! Now's not the time to chat with Alan! Catria thought.

"Argh, let me, go!" cried the angel.

"Khhhh! Kill! Kill! Kill the angel!"

"But first, violate! How many times I say, idiot?!"

"Gonna keeeel *yooouuu*!"

The demons seemed to be scuffling over their disturbing kinks.

This was Catria's chance! She drew her Holy Knight Blade. "Lady Angel, I shall lend you my sword!"

"Huh?! A human?! How could a mortal come this far?!" The angel looked puzzled, but she soon shook her head. "No, that matters not! You must run! You cannot hope to defeat these foul beasts!"

"I'll be okay! More importantly, close your eyes, Lady Angel!"

"Huh?"

Catria gathered holy energy at the tip of her sword. No matter what anyone told her, it was *holy* energy. *Not* shovel energy. As proof, the white energy she summoned was in the shape of a cross.

Defeat the demons! That was what this holy aura was telling Catria. Or at least, it sure felt like it to her. (In reality, the aura was actually making digging sounds, but hey. It was what it was.)

The important thing here was to power through. Catria had to trick herself into believing this had nothing to do with shovels.

"GOOOOO! JUSTICE STREAM!!!"

KA-CHOOOOOOOOM!

Catria's Justice Stream (she named it herself) enveloped and incinerated the demons. All that remained when the light dissipated was the totally unharmed angel.

I did it! I fired it again! My Justice Stream killed the demons!

"Yaaaay! Catria, that was an amazing Wave Motion Shovel Blast!"

"No it wasn't! It was my Holy Wave Blade's Justice Stream!"

"But your sword changed into a shovel."

"Huh?"

Catria looked down to find her Holy Knight Blade was now a Holy Knight Shovel. She gazed at it in complete silence, then threw it to the ground with all the power she had.

CLANK!

On impact, it changed form back into a sword. Destruction of incriminating evidence complete.

"Your Highness, what are you talking about? This is a Holy Knight Blade."

"You buried the truth with your shovel... You've truly become shovependable."

"It's a Holy Knight Blade!" Catria said with a smile, her tone of voice desperate as hell.

"You, your name is Catria, no? More importantly, your sword!" The angel descended before them. She grabbed Catria's hands, her eyes alight with hope. "My word! This is truly a Holy Blade! Proof that you are a real hero!"

"Huh? O-oh, yes, of course! This is a bona fide Holy Knight Blade!"

This was crazy! Catria and her weapon had been recognized by a real angel. This here was incontrovertible proof she wielded a genuine Holy Knight Blade. Her chest burned hot. The princess was the one in the wrong! She was a hero! A holy hero! HA HA!

"Oh, Great Hero Catria. What god graced you with this Holy Blade?!"

Time stopped. Catria wanted to answer that her sword had been entrusted to her by the greatest deity of them all, the high Sun God, but she couldn't. She was a Holy Knight. She could lie to herself, but not to an angel. That would be unforgivable.

"Well, er..."

"Please tell me! Depending on your answer, I have a sworn duty to serve you!"

An Angel Knight, serving Catria? Catria couldn't help but tremble with excitement. But the Holy Knight nonetheless swallowed her words. She couldn't lie. She couldn't betray her enduring sense of justice.

"This sword was crafted by the miner over there, Lady Angel."

"Excuse me?" The angel glanced at Alan's back and the shovel strapped across it. She laughed. "Ah ha ha ha ha! Not a bad joke for a human!"

"I spent many days wishing it was a joke, but it's the truth."

"Great Hero Catria, I ask that you take this seriously. The magic embedded in that sword could not have been handled by a human. That much is certain. It must have been enchanted by the Mining God Areus, or..."

"No." Lithisia interrupted the angel. "It was the God of Shovels, Lady Angel."

Lithisia had been biting her lip, her expression somewhat frustrated. She had wanted to hold herself back, but once her beloved miner was brushed off, all bets were off.

"Sir Miner is the God of Shovels. How could you possibly call yourself an angel without knowing that?"

"Pardon?! Wh-who is this woman and what is wrong with her, Great Hero Catria?"

"As much as I agree something is deeply wrong with her, she's my master."

The angel's face faulted into sympathy. "Great Hero Catria, your struggles must have been long and hard."

"They...have," Catria replied with a straight face.

The angel placed her hand on her forehead and sighed. "Human princess, let me teach you the ways of this world. A shovel is naught but a simple mining tool. Gods do not preside over such trite objects. They govern the great, entities such as the vast ocean, the stars, the sun. These are the objects worth the attention of the gods. Do you understand?"

The angel's patient lecture was powerfully convincing. However, Lithisia's smile remained unchanged.

"Wonderful summary, Lady Angel. As thanks, allow me to explain as well." Lithisia's eyes shone with a suspicious light. "Allow me to explain the ways of this universe to you."

"Wha?"

This angel's done for, Catria thought to herself.

They were interrupted by the whoosh of distant wings. Far away in the sky, a pulsing mass of black shadows approached. It was an aerial unit of demons numbering in the hundreds, perhaps more. The angel gasped in panic.

"This is terrible, truly awful! An army of demons! Great Hero Catria, gather your allies and flee into one of the nearby buildings!"

"Lady Angel, there's no need to flee," Catria assured her.

"Please, listen to me! As powerful as you might be, even you stand no chance against a horde like that!"

"Well, no, but I'm not the one who's going to fight them."

"Excuse me?"

Catria looked to Alan. Until a moment ago, he had been directing his attention to the skies. Now he was holding his shovel above his head as it collected a shining aura of blue energy. Catria's own abilities paled in comparison to the violence with which his shovel gathered more and more power. It was like a storm. A tempest.

Catria recalled the words of the angel—how only someone nonhuman could fire off something like a Holy Knight Blade.

I think she wasn't wrong.

"DIG!"

Alan fired his Wave Motion Shovel Blast.

KA-CHOOOOOOOOM!

Its diameter was at least ten thousand times that of Catria's beam, its destructive force one million times more powerful, and its impact a trillion times greater. Alan's Wave Motion Shovel Blast blew the demon army to pieces and sent them flying in all directions.

Bleh. This guy ain't human.

"Uh, um, er, wha?" The angel's mouth was agape. Catria didn't know if angels had pupils or what, but they were probably dilated.

Lithisia offered her words of gratitude to Alan, as always. She then turned to the Angel and smiled. "Lady Angel, do you understand now how the universe works?"

The angel was breathless and the color of her eyes was... wrong. Perhaps as a side effect of the Wave Motion Shovel Blast, they were now purple. All of her basic knowledge of the universe had been rewritten in an instant, or at least that was what it seemed like.

When Lithisia saw this, she offered her red shovel to the sky like she was trying to scoop up the sun itself. In an inviting voice, she whispered, "Greater than the great ocean! Greater than the sun itself. The shovel is the greatest of them all, shovel! ...Ow!"

Alan bopped Lithisia on the head. "Cut it out. Stop trying to Shovel Brainwash the angel while she's still stunned by my beam."

"Owie...I'm sorry. I just wanted a guardian angel for our Holy Shovel Faith..."

"I don't need one of those."

Catria let out a deep sigh. She'd seen more than enough. Alan had blasted the angel's common sense to smithereens, and now Lithisia was trying to mind control her. She was done with it all.

But Catria was most fed up with herself for feeling like Lithisia's words had any sort of weight or truth.

PART 32
The Miner Shovels an Archangel

WITH THE ANGEL IN TOW, Alan and his party entered one of Rahzelfo's grand buildings. In the center of an open room was a table made from some sort of mysterious black material. It appeared as though the ancients used this room as a conference hall. Currently, the angel, Alan, Catria, and Lithisia were occupying it. Alice was still down for the count at one of the rest stops after that earlier vigorous shoveling.

"Now then, let's start again from the top." The angel cleared her throat and turned to Catria. "My name is Lucy. I am an angel who serves the Pantheon of the Sun. They have charged me with watching over the world below."

"Pantheon of the Sun?"

This was an unfamiliar set of words. Catria hadn't learned of any such thing during her holy studies.

A kind smile crossed Lucy's face. "It makes sense that you know not of them. They are the basis of all gods, and a divine mystery to the human world. Now, where shall I begin..."

"A Pantheon is basically like a faction, Catria," Alan cut in. "As you know, there's way more than one god—we've got a whole bunch of them. For example, the Sun God and the Star God. The most powerful among them start Pantheons where they gather gods related to the stuff they rule over. For example, the Sun God might recruit the Solar Eclipse God or the Dawn God. In human terms, they become a faction."

Catria nodded. Alan's explanation was easy to follow and made absolute sense. It was basically the same thing as when knights went to serve under a lord or master.

"Wonderful, Sir God Miner! Your shovel knowledge is on level with that of the gods!" Lithisia declared.

"Don't call me that."

"W-wait just a second!" Lucy panicked and cut in. Her wings were shivering. "How does a human know about the Pantheons?!"

"Oh, I heard about them from an Angel Knight who'd been imprisoned in Hell."

Alan held up his shovel as he described the experience of coming upon that deep, dark prison.

As Alan used his shovel to delve into his mountain, at one point he inadvertently connected his mining route to Hell itself. He soon found a winged angel who had been captured by the forces of Hell, then stripped and tortured in their cell. Their wings had darkened and they were on the verge of becoming a fallen angel.

After Alan saved the angel with his shovel, they extended an invitation to him. "Oh, great hero! We would welcome you in our Pantheon of the Earth!"

In other words, a Pantheon for gods related to the Earth God.

Of course, Alan declined the invitation. If he were to become a god, he wouldn't be able to just wander around mining for precious stones. The rescued angel seemed terribly disappointed by the rejection, but they eventually gave up and flew away.

"And that's how I learned about Pantheons."

"Wait, wait, this is ludicrous. Where do I even begin?!" Lucy's face twisted and contorted as her breathing turned rough.

There were so many unbelievable things about Alan's tale. First of all, getting to Hell via shovel was impossible, not to mention saving an angel imprisoned there. What the heck? All while digging for regular old obsidian? None of this made any kind of angelic sense!

"C-Catria! You mustn't allow yourself to grow close to a liar such as he!"

"I 100 percent completely agree with you, I really do. Painfully so. But..."

"Catria, are you right of mind?!"

"Lady Angel, you saw this guy's Wave Motion Shovel Blast, didn't you?"

Lucy's words stuck in her throat. That Wave Motion Shovel Blast was certainly no mortal technique. Lucy had seen only one similar such move in her life: the Divine Blast the Sun God used to destroy the Evil God. The level of power was different, but the form and light had been identical.

No, this was impossible! Lucy shook her head until she was dizzy. There was no way a human could learn a technique like that and still retain their humanity. "This has to be a trick of some kind!"

Catria found herself feeling quite bad for the angel. Despite Lucy's heavenly nature, even she struggled to understand Alan.

"P-plus, Catria! His story includes a vital contradiction!"

"Really?"

"Once an angel's wings darken, there's no coming back!"

Because angels were born from holy energies, they were so pure that they were easy to corrupt. However, once their wings, the source of their holiness, were darkened, there was no way to save them. Corruption spread fast and permanently.

Lucy wore a victorious expression as she pointed a finger at Alan. "As such, you are nothing but a liar!"

"Exshovel me (anger)?"

"Calm down, Lithisia. Put your shovel away. I'm not upset."

"Shovel..." Lithisia muttered.

Even though he'd been called a liar to his face, Alan was unshaken. He wasn't out to seek the favor of this angel. In fact, if he could help it, he'd actively avoid it. It'd be a pain to get invited to a Pantheon again.

"More importantly, I'd like to discuss Rahzelfo," he said.

"Mmph—fine. Let us begin."

Lucy explained she had descended upon Rahzelfo from the heavens above because her Pantheon had received intelligence that a group of high-ranking demons were planning a large-scale invasion on the world below. She and her sister Gabriella were the vanguard sent by the gods. Furthermore, Gabriella was an archangel, a powerful figure to say the least.

After some investigation, they found their intelligence was accurate, and not only that, the situation was far more dire than they anticipated. The Emperor of the Sky, Pazuzu, was leading an army of demons in an attempt to open Hell's Gate.

"Huh, is that what Zeleburg is after?"

Hell's Gate connected the surface world to Hell. If something like that were to be opened, humanity would be in grave danger.

"Lady Angel, will the gods not act?" asked Catria.

"If the gods were to do so, the God of Evil would as well."

The forces of good and evil were locked in a standstill that prevented either side from moving recklessly.

"Well, I think I just about understand the situation," said Alan. "I have one question."

"Is that so? Go ahead. I will only answer with the truth, unlike a certain lying shovel man."

"Exshovel me (anger)?!"

"Lithisia, stand down. According to your words, Gabriella is an archangel, correct? Where is she?"

Lucy did a terrifically poor job of hiding her response, tearing up at his words. "My sister Gabriella is, uh..."

Lucy looked down, then weakly shook her head. Catria was all too familiar with her body language. It was that of someone drowning in their own uselessness.

"In order to give me a chance to escape, she...she fought the demons off... She was captured. She's probably already in Hell..."

"Lady Angel..."

"Do not pity me, Great Hero Catria. This is the fate of all Angel Knights." Lucy wiped the tears from her eyes and smiled valiantly.

"So you're saying she's imprisoned in Hell?"

"Vanguards from Heaven captured by demons are inevitably tortured in their dark prison."

Catria looked to Alan. He nodded with a simple confidence.

"Right then. I'll save her with my shovel."

"Wha?"

In a split second, Alan left Rahzelfo and descended to the World Tree Castle. Fio was surprised to see him, but he explained he had some business to take care of in Hell. From there, he began his infiltration of the deep. It took him thirty seconds to descend the 6,666,666 steps leading to Hell and arrive at a particular cell within the magma-ridden landscape.

Gabriella was right where he'd suspected she would be. She had a similar aura to Lucy, but her strength was on another level. She had also been stripped and her body showed clear signs of torture. Furthermore, Her beautiful black hair was ragged and unevenly cut.

Alan called out to the miserable woman. "I'm here to save you, Gabriella."

"Ah... Huh?"

Alan eliminated the demon guarding Gabriella's cell with a short Wave Motion Shovel Blast and used his shovel to undo Gabriella's bindings. He scooped up the naked Gabriella (she had a heavenly figure) and held her like a princess. Cradling her delicate form, he made his way back up the stairs of Hell, had a spot of tea with Fio, dropped in on Alice, and promptly returned to Rahzelfo with Gabriella in tow.

The entire journey took him approximately one minute and twenty-eight seconds, break time included. He actually set the record for the fastest marathon from Heaven to Hell.

"Hey there, I've saved Gabriella," he said. With that, he presented Lucy with her older sister.

"HOOOOOLD UP!" Lucy finally screamed. *What in blue blazes is going on?! How can Gabriella be here?! What the shovel?!*

But the fact of the matter was that Lucy's beloved Gabriella was lying at her feet, and she was the same beautiful angel Lucy had always striven to be like.

"Lady Angel, I truly understand how confused you must be, but let us first tend to Lady Gabriella's wounds," said Catria.

"Ah! Y-you're right! Gabriella, hang in there!"

"Ah...urgh...Lucy...?" Gabriella's breath was labored, but she was conscious. Needless to say, she was in awful condition. Wounds covered her entire body, and her wings were in tatters.

Worse, Lucy caught sight of a tip of one of Gabriella's wings and raised her voice in despair. "My beloved sister, no, it can't be! Your wings!"

They were beginning to blacken. Gabriella was falling into darkness.

"Oh my..." In response to Lucy's voice, Gabriella glanced at the tip of her darkened wing. The archangel smiled. "Lucy...take up your sword..."

"What?!"

Without breaking her proud smile, Gabriella continued. "Thank you so much for saving me... I truly am blessed...I get to die as an angel..."

"Gabriella, I...!" Tears fell from Lucy's eyes. *No, this can't be!*

But it was already too late. Gabriella's darkening had begun. From here on out, Gabriella's very existence would corrupt. The "Dark Pleasure of a Fallen Angel" would soon paint even her heart pitch-black. The only way to stop this from happening was to cut off her wings, thereby destroying her.

"Lucy, you must do your duty as an Angel Knight."

"Ngh...!"

Just as Lucy swung her sword with trembling hands—Catria grabbed her arm.

"Great Hero Catria?!"

"This is really hard for me to say, but, um, your sister is probably going to be fine."

"Catria... No, it's too late. Once an angel's wings corrupt even the smallest bit..."

"No, really, it's gonna be okay. Right, Alan?" Catria turned to the miner.

Alan gripped his shovel and sighed. "Ugh. I'd rather not get into it, but I suppose this is an emergency. Guess I've got no choice."

Catria internally sighed. Despair was meaningless in front of Alan. As for why, well, he simply rejected the word time and time again.

"FILL!"

Alan stabbed his shovel into Gabriella's wings and the darkened tips were wrapped in a rush of light. It was true that Alan couldn't eliminate the corruption within her wings. However, if he could bury within them a large enough quantity of light that it overwhelmed the quantity of corruption...

Gabriella's body shone with awe-inspiring incandescence,

so much so that all Lucy could do was watch, mouth agape. Eventually the light faded, revealing a Gabriella with pure white wings.

"Huh? But... I..."

"There we go. That went about as well as it could've," said Alan.

"Amazing heavenly scoop! (Amazing! You retrieved and saved the angel!)"

"You really need to keep a lid on that stream of consciousness of yours, Lithisia."

Gabriella glanced at her surroundings. For some reason, even her wounds had been healed.

Tears continued to stream from Lucy's eyes. *I can't believe it, but she's right here... This isn't a trick. She's still a pure white angel!*

"My dear sister, you're okay!"

As Lucy rushed over to gather her sister in her arms, Gabriella's expression turned to that of bafflement. "I...I... was I shovel saved, shovel?"

Lucy halted just before embracing her sister.

Catria did her best to hold back her oncoming headache. Gabriella the archangel was smiling, and for some reason her cheeks were in high color. Upon closer inspection, her pupils had taken the form of triangles...shovels, to be exact.

"Alan, is it just me, or did you do something to this poor angel with your shovel?!"

"All I did was fire off my Shovel Light and overwrite her corrupted energy."

"She sure seems plenty corrupted to me."

"Don't worry, she'll be fine. At worst, her eyes, language, and consciousness will suffer some side effects."

"None of that qualifies as fine!"

"I was even careful to limit the corruption. If I had messed up, her name might've suffered from a Shovel Error."

"Amazingly shoveltastic, Sir Miner!" Lithisia was moved.

With her shovel-shaped pupils shining, Gabriella drew close to Lucy. "Lucy, what's wrong? It's me, the archangel Gabriella, shovel."

"Please get a hold of yourself, Gabriella! Why do you keep saying shovel?!"

"I'm perfectly of shovel sound mind."

It was almost like there were two Princess Lithisias.

Lucy shook as she leveled her holy sword at Alan. "You bastard... What did you do to my beloved sister?! You treacherous demon!"

"Don't worry. In about a hundred years, she should lose most of her shovel edge."

So you're telling me she'll still have some shovel corruption even after one hundred years? I refuse to ever let him do that to me, Catria thought bleakly.

"Do not test my patience!!!" Without warning, Lucy came slashing at Alan.

Gabriella swooped forward, catching Lucy's hand. "What are you doing? Stop this at once, Lucy! This man saved my life, shovel!"

"Let me go! This bastard...he...he...!"

"You appear to be rather frazzled... In that case, I have no choice, shovel." Gabriella snapped her fingers.

A rope resembling the halo above an angel's head appeared and snaked around Lucy, binding her in place.

"Gah! Gabriella...!"

The older sister was clearly the stronger of the two.

"I must apologize for my beloved sister's poor shovel behavior. Please forgive her," said Gabriella with a bow.

"This angel's not too bad at all! She's mixing 'shovel' into her sentences like it's no big deal!" Lithisia cheered.

"Quiet, Lithisia," said Alan, and turned to Gabriella. "And look, there's nothing to forgive. I'm not upset."

Gabriella offered her gratitude with grace befitting her divinity, but as she did, she noticed she was still in the buff. Embarrassment crossed her face and she promptly tried to cover her indecencies as best she could. "I'm so sorry. I didn't mean to show you my shovelly body..."

"She's already using it as an adjective?!" Lithisia gasped.

"Lithisia, I'm begging you here, go to sleep. More importantly, how are you feeling, Gabriella?"

"Um, well... Could I receive permission to go back to Heaven and report what you've done for me?"

Alan frowned. *Hrm, her body is fine, but she's definitely suffering from some side effects.*

Lucy in the meantime continued to cry, inconsolably devastated.

"Sir Human, I wish to leave Lucy here for further reconnaissance. Is it all right if she remains with you?" Gabriella asked.

"I'm fine with it, but I'm not so sure she is."

Lucy looked as though she wanted to tear Alan apart with her teeth. Her bloodlust was palpable.

"That's certainly a shovel problem... In that case." Gabriella slid a ring off of her finger and handed it to Alan. "Lucy must obey the person who wears this 'Heavenly Shovel Ring.' It was given to me for this mission."

"The name is rather odd."

"It used to be referred to as the 'Ring of the Archangel,' but I have changed it. Please try not to lose it."

"NNGH! (BELOVED SISTER, PLEASE, PLEASE SNAP OUT OF IT!)"

"Lucy, this being before you is a truly great human. You are the one who needs to snap out of it, shovel."

And so Gabriella once again offered her gratitude while deftly concealing her breasts, then flew into the sky. Of course, she left behind Lucy, who was currently bound in heavenly rope and looking like the heroine of a pulpy tragedy.

"All right. Time to find that orb. You lead the way, Lucy."

"NO! I refuse! Why should I have to—ngh?!"

Alan's ring flared with holy radiance, and Lucy jolted as if she had been shocked with electricity.

"EEEEK! Th-this way, please...augh!" Lucy turned to Catria, her expression pleading for any kind of salvation. *Save me. Turn my sister back to normal. Please.*

The angel's gaze was desperation itself. Unfortunately, Catria averted her eyes.

"All right. Let's go, Alan."

"GREAT HERO CATRIA?!"

Yeah, so, uh, my bad. Catria grimaced, unable to face the angel. *Just chalk it up to bad luck and give up on your sister. I mean, your whole situation is scarily similar to the horrors I endured myself. Gabriella is...*

"Sir Miner, Sir Miner! I'm going as well! I'll accompany you no matter how shovelly far you shovelly go!"

"Stop inserting 'shovel' into random places just to make yourself look better than Gabriella."

"Shovel..."

Gabriella is long gone, just like Princess Lithisia.

ACCORDING TO THE ANGEL LUCY, in order to reach the center of Rahzelfo, they would first have to acquire the Elemental Keys. These were kept within the Towers of the Four Elements located at the far corners of the city. Although Lucy was an angel, like the rest of her kind, descending to the physical plane bound her to the laws of physics. The challenges contained within the Towers would be as daunting for her as for any fleshly being.

As for Catria, when she heard of these Towers she thought, *Ah, this is the part where Alan just destroys all common sense and physics.*

"H-hmph! As if a lying shovel human like you could ever collect all the Elemental Keys!" Lucy's eyes were filled with tears as she stared defiantly at Alan. Since witnessing her sister's descent into shovelhood, her level of trust in this man had likewise plummeted far past zero. "I'll never forgive you for what you've done!"

"You mean your sister? You know, if I'd left her as she was, she would've fallen into darkness."

"Argh!" Lucy swallowed her words.

Alan was right. An angel whose wings darkened could never return to the heavenly host. That was *supposed* to be a fact. But presently, reality defied facts. Gabriella's wings had been restored to their old pure white and had even emanated the same transcendental aura they once had. If Gabriella had fallen, the change in her manner of speech and aura would've been readily apparent. So in that sense, Alan really was Lucy's sister's savior... He was, but...!

"Even so! I...I...I will never forgive you!"

Lucy would never forgive Alan for dragging her sister, an archangel, into the unholy depths of shovelhood.

"Sir Miner, shall we shovel up this bratty little angel? We have complete control over her mind and body, after all."

"Ngh?!" Lucy immediately covered her breasts and exposed thighs, shaken by the princess's words. However, she soon forced out a smile and chuckled. "Aha! But if you were to issue an evil command, the ring would explode!"

"Hrm, really?"

"Yes, really. That ring is designed to assist an archangel in all of their duties. If it senses any manner of misuse, it immediately detonates."

Alan examined the Holy Shovel Ring, which now sat on his middle finger. It was an exquisite thing, inscribed with feathers and a shining diamond.

SHING! A vertical transparent window displaying numbers and text suddenly appeared next to Lucy.

Alan frowned. "What the heck is that?"

For some reason, Lucy curled up on herself a bit, flustered. "Urgh, p-probably my status window."

"Status?"

"It is part of an archangel's duty to raise and cultivate the angels working below them. The ring allows them to assess the status of said angels."

Perhaps due to the effects of the ring, Lucy truthfully explained how everything worked.

"And that's all converted into numeric values, eh? This'd be useful for cultivating my successor." Alan inspected the window more closely.

Angel Lucy (Pantheon of the Sun)

CLASS: Rank 8, Lesser Angel

THREE SIZES: 35, 21, 32

CORRUPTION: No Experience

SKILL (MAX 10): Heavenly Swordsmanship (Lv 2)
Divine Magic (Lv 1) Madness Resistance (Lv 1)

TITLE: Angel Cub

CULTIVATION NOTES: Average potential, fairly impulsive, overly confident. Training will be a struggle. Gabriella's little sister. As such, we expect (and pray) her abilities will increase in the future.

"..."

Who wrote her title? And those notes? They didn't seem like the kind of things Gabriella would say. Angels could be rather tough on each other...

"Well? Impressed by our heavenly technology?" asked Lucy.

"If anything, I'm a little perplexed by the details," said Alan.

What was the point of the "three sizes" business? Also, what the hell did "corruption" mean?

The god who made this system was kind of a (shovel censored), thought Alan. "I guess the data appears to be... accurate."

Lucy's face was girlish, but her diaphanous robes barely contained her sizable chest. She wasn't as busty as Fio, but she was a close competitor. Her short skirt flapped in the least breeze, and frankly was wildly inappropriate, considering how often she flew through the air. This rendered her thighs unfortunately distracting.

Under the glare of inspection, Lucy couldn't help but hide her chest with her arms. "Wh-what are you staring at?! You filthy man!"

"I was just confirming the accuracy of the data. Don't you know what your profile says?"

"So what if I don't? Did...something surprise you?"

Gabriella apparently hadn't explained what came up in that window. Was it really okay for Alan to spill the beans? ...No, probably not. For the time being, he would close the window. He brought his hand over the "X" button in the upper right-hand corner.

As he did, the window moved. It seemed the window shifted in relation to the position of the ring. As such, Alan accidentally pressed the "transmit to person in question" button next to the "X."

Who the heck designed this interface? It's so unsafe!

"Ah, this is my status..." Lucy was stock-still as she stared at the window floating in front of her. She blinked multiple times, her mouth opened and closed, and her eyes darted about.

Huh? What is this? Am I dreaming? Is this a shovel? Why are my three sizes...and this evaluation... This has to be wrong! Right, Catria?

Lucy looked to the female knight like an abandoned kitten.

After mulling for a moment, Catria patted her shoulder. "Well, you know... Let's both do our best, Lucy."

"GREAT HERO CATRIA?!"

At this outburst, Catria felt an intense camaraderie with the angel.

She gets it. Huh, I guess there are all kinds of angels out there.

Just as a wave of relief washed over Catria, Alan pumped himself up.

"Angel cultivating, eh? Since Gabriella left me in charge, I've gotta do my best."

A chill ran down Catria's spine. She already knew how this was going to end. *Probably the same thing that happened to me...*

On the eastern side of the city was one of the Four Elemental Towers, the Flame Tower. It was twenty stories tall with deep scarlet walls, and it spat blistering flame and sweltering heat from various points along them. It would be a trial just getting to the entrance.

Lucy coughed repeatedly. "Ugh, it's scorching!"

"Hrm, so even angels are weak against fire?"

"Greater Angels have flame resistance, but...urgh."

While Lucy spoke, she realized Alan, Lithisia, and Catria all appeared perfectly fine as they approached the Tower.

"W-wait just a second! Why are you *humans* all right?!"

"By digging up space with a shovel, I can cut off the heat."

"I'll follow you to the ends of the shovel, Sir Miner!"

Crap, I unconsciously followed along with the same logic as the princess! Catria faked heavy breathing. "I'm hot too, Lucy! We're the same!"

"Oh my, so we are, Great Hero Catria..." Lucy's peace was short-lived. "Wait...when did you start calling me by my name?!"

"You're imagining things. I've been calling you Lucy since the very beginning."

"Oh, I guess I must be mistaken. My apologies..."

This angel was tragically easy to manipulate.

"How about I teach you flame resistance, Lucy?" asked Alan.

"Pardon?"

Alan brought his shovel down in front of Lucy and wiggled it to and fro. Lucy followed it with her eyes, which went glassy. Her breathing steadied. Proper breathing calms the heart, you see. What's more, Lucy was Gabriella's little sister; she learned fast.

Soon, Alan smacked his shovel against the ground. With the sound, life returned to Lucy's eyes.

"Okay, Lucy. Come here, but keep your breathing steady."

"Huh? N-no, I'm going to get burned...!"

But due to the complete control the ring gave Alan, Lucy could do naught but obey as her body moved toward the flames. To her surprise, even once she stood beside the searing fire, she still felt totally cool.

"Whaaaa?!"

Just then, a strange ding echoed. Lucy's window automatically appeared and in the Skill column, "Calm the Heart, Calm the Flames Shovelly (SHV Lv3)," appeared.

Lithisia was newly impressed by the use-value of that window, but Lucy cried out.

"What the heck is this skill?!" she wailed. "And what does 'SHV Lv 3' mean?!"

"Resistance against flames via sturdy breathing. SHV Lv stands for Shovel Level, I imagine."

"Nooooooooooo!" Lucy cried. She'd been corrupted. Despite being an angel, she had been tainted. *My Skill column's been defiled...!*

Lucy moaned in despair and Catria supported her by the shoulders.

"Lucy, you have to get a grip."

"Ah, Great Hero Catria...will you save me from this horror?!"

"Of course. I'll do anything within my power (because it'd be a huge problem for me if I lost one of the few people with a grasp on basic logic)."

"Catria...!"

Catria would do what she could, but in reality, that probably wasn't much. She could only hope the angel's Madness Resistance held out.

Ten seconds later, Alan had entered the Flame Tower and used his shovel to remodel the interior until it was completely safe. He then ordered Lucy to head to the top of the Tower and retrieve the Flame Key. Once Lucy had cut through the sea of magma blocking the path and returned to the party, her Shovel Level had risen from three to five.

Lucy collapsed on the floor with her legs splayed. "It should be hot, but it's not... But my tears, they're scalding...Catria!"

Lucy brought her thighs together tightly and sobbed, her wings drooping.

"Hang in there, Lucy. I'm with you!"

"Ah, Great Hero Catria...!"

Ring a ding ding!

Just like that, Lucy's Madness Resistance rose to Level 2. In some ways, she might've been happier without this resistance. Or so Catria thought. She sympathized, but in the end, sympathy didn't amount to much.

"Next up is the Wind Tower to the west."

"Tally shovel!"

"That one was really forced, Lithisia."

"Shorry..."

"No, it's... Well, whatever. Do what you want."

"Will, Shovel."

Next, the party made their way to the Wind Tower. As per its name, the building itself was surrounded by violent gusts of wind. The storm enveloping it was so fierce, in fact, they couldn't get anywhere near. As such, Alan held up his shovel, howled "FILL!" and raised a wall from the ground that totally blocked the screaming winds. Instant physical wall protection.

"This is shovelpossible!"

"Be strong, Lucy. Your words are falling apart! That's the first dark sign of shovelfication!"

"What?!" Lucy's glossy pink hair shook back and forth as life returned to her eyes. "Ah, Catria. Please, please stay by my side and protect me from the evil shovel!"

"I don't know if I can do that, but I can at least be with you through it all."

Once the team entered the Wind Tower, they were met with another fierce storm. Like usual, Alan used his Wave Motion Shovel Blast to power his way through. At the very top of the Tower was the Wind Key, and just like before, he shovel hypnotized Lucy into retrieving it.

"Scoop up the wind...scoop up the wind...scoop up the Wind!"

Lucy flapped her wings at cosmic speeds.

"Whaaaaa?!"

Ring a ding ding!

On her return from fetching the Wind Key, Lucy acquired the "Shovel Flight (SHV Lv3)" skill in her Skill column. Being an angel and all, it did make sense she'd be good at flying.

At this, Lucy hugged Catria tightly, pressing her breasts up against the lady knight as she sobbed. Yet in spite of her tears, her wings remained a luminous pure white.

"Catria... My wings have been defiled by the shovel... completely and utterly defiled, but they're still white!"

"Ah, don't worry, Lucy! They still look like ordinary wings! They're not shaped like shovels or anything!"

"What do you mean by 'still'?! Are they going to turn into shovels?!"

A moment of silence.

"Alan, let's make way for the Earth Tower."

"Right."

"NOOOOOOOOOOO!!!"

And thus the party arrived at the Earth Tower, a building near entirely encased within a mountain. As usual, Alan diligently cultivated Lucy's talents, enabling her to acquire "Earth Blade Skill (SHV Lv 3)." This was a sword skill that allowed her to use an earth-shoveling motion paired with Heavenly Blade Skills.

"L-Look, Lucy! The name's cool and everything! Check out the skill name!" cried Catria.

"But it still has a SHV Lv! Angelic skills are supposed to be holy!" cried Lucy.

"The shovel *is* holy!" cried Lithisia.

"Eeek! Humans are terrifying! I'm scared, Catria..."

"Hang in there, Lucy! That thing isn't a human!"

"How disreshovelful! (How disrespectful. I am in fact a human. Don't make me shovel you.)"

"And I'm trying to tell you no human talks or acts like that, Your Highness!"

Following this, Lucy had no trouble obtaining the Earth Key, though after she was on all fours, staring blankly at the ground with no tears left to shed.

I'm so sorry, Gabriella. I can't save you... I've been

corrupted. My skills, my wings, my blade...I'm a failure of an angel. I deserve to be exiled from the heavens!

Just then, a valiant fanfare played from high above.

"Huh?" Lucy stared.

There was a change to her status window. Her class had gone up to "Rank 7: Intermediate Angel." Also, her title was now "Fair Angel."

"Wait, but, what?"

"Huh, so an angel's class changes based on what sort of skills they acquire and how they level." Alan nodded thoughtfully.

But Lucy didn't quite follow. This couldn't be true. Classes didn't rank up so simply. Gabriella had risen in the ranks of the host far more swiftly than any angel in history, but even she took five years to reach Rank 3, that of "archangel." More often angels took fifteen or twenty years to do the same, and many took even longer.

Heck, Lucy had spent ten years as a Rank 8 angel. And yet in just a few minutes, she had already gone up a rank? That was impossible!

"GRAAAAAH! Eliminate, angels...!" snarled a beastly voice.

It came from a mountainous golem who grew from the ruins of the Tower. This was likely the guardian of the Earth Tower. Alan hefted his shovel but didn't otherwise move, instead looking to Catria and Lucy. He intended to leave this task to them.

"Whoa, wait just a second! You want the two of us to take on that thing?!" said Catria.

Catria might have defeated a few of the Hydra's tentacles, but this golem was a hundred times crazier. And judging by what she'd seen of Lucy's strength, the angel was likely on par with Catria and her fledgling beam weapon.

"Don't worry. As far as I can tell, you and Lucy together should be able to handle the golem."

"What?!"

As they argued, the golem lumbered closer. One way or another, they would have to fight. Catria grit her teeth and turned to face the hulking guardian. She unleashed her most powerful attack: Justice Stream.

A wave beam of light erupted from the tip of her blade and struck the golem's head, but the monstrous guardian didn't stop. Its Stopping Power (not Shoveling Power) was too high.

"GRAAAAAAAAAAAHHH!!!" Catria shouted in an attempt to focus her beam.

Lucy watched this from the side, dithering. *This isn't right. I should help. Catria has stuck by me through thick and thin.*

Actually, now that she thought about it, "sticking around" was all Catria had ever done. Nonetheless, her "savior" was in danger. As a guardian angel, she had to save her hero. But how?

That's when Alan cried out, "Now, Lucy! FIRE!"

"Huh?!"

Fire what?! I don't have any projectile weapons!

Even so, Lucy was compelled to obey Alan's orders, so her body moved on its own. She flapped her wings until she hovered in the air and raised both hands toward the heavens. Suddenly, a sparkling spear appeared just over her head. It shimmered as if it were harmonizing with Catria's holy waves.

"What's happening?!" Lucy stared at the spear in disbelief. This was her big sister's...Gabriella's special move... And then the words left Lucy's mouth. "HOLY LANCE!"

KA-CHOOOOOOOOM!

The beam of light flew through the air. It was at least equal to Catria's Justice Stream, if not more brilliant in terms of light. The heavenly projectile pierced the golem, which proceeded to crumble into pieces.

There was no doubt Lucy had just used the Holy Lance, a move only Greater Angels could hope to pull off.

"Haaah, haaah. You did it, Lucy!"

As soon as the angel returned to the ground, she was welcomed by Catria. Lucy stared at her own hands in shock.

Alan nodded. "Perfect. Looks like this whole angel cultivation thing has been successful."

"Amazing sheavenly taming! (I knew Sir Miner could train even an angel!)"

"It wasn't taming, it was raising. Cultivating her talents."

Lucy's heart raced within her chest. Her heart only existed in an astral sense, and yet it was beating a mile a minute. She was certain she would be exiled from the heavens. She feared she would be corrupted by the shovel. Yet despite all that had been done to her, all she had been forced to do, her angelic rank had increased. Now, she could use the same expert move as her beloved older sister. And above all else, in her status window under "corruption" it still read "no experience."

Lucy shot Alan a fierce look brimming with passion. She was still full of questions and doubt, but within her an even more powerful sense of trust had been born.

Could it be that this man...that Gabriella was right about him? That he truly is a great...

Ring a ding ding!

That was the sound of Lucy acquiring yet another skill. Lucy immediately checked her window.

"Holy Lanshovel (SHV Lv 3)."

"..."

Thunk, thunk, thunk.

This was the sound of Lucy's reason crumbling to pieces.

"Perfect, you've acquired a new skill... What's wrong, Lucy?"

Sploosh!

This was the sound of Lucy's tears as they came flooding from her eyes like a waterfall.

"You...you shovel demon! Give me back my honor and respect!"

"Whoa!"

"I'll never forgive you! Never, ever, ever!" Lucy's breasts bounced as she jabbed at Alan. She'd hit her breaking point.

Simultaneously, Lithisia's veins throbbed with rage.

Catria panicked and cut in before things could go completely off the rails. "No, Lucy! I understand how you feel, but you have to keep yourself together. You're gonna get yourself shoveled!"

"I hate this! Great Hero Catria, help me... Please, I beg of you! I can't take this anymore!"

"Grrr..."

"Catria, it's all going to be okay. I have an idea!" Lithisia whispered in Catria's ear.

"Oh, right!" Catria turned her hand toward the status window. A holy aura pulsed from her Holy Knight Blade as she pointed it at the Skill column. With burning white light, Catria buried part of the text.

"Holy Lans e (Lv3)."

Sure, the spelling was off, and there were some unnatural spaces here and there, but other than that, it was perfect!

"Look, Lucy! You really did wield the 'Holy Lanse'!" said Catria.

"You must've been seeing things as a side effect of the shovel shock," said Lithisia.

"Really?! Ah, th-thank goodness..." said Lucy as she trembled with emotion.

Catria sheathed her sword and sighed. *If I lose any more decent-minded companions, I'm going to be the next one to lose my mind. Thank goodness I buried those characters in white... Wait. Isn't that strange?*

Catria thought for a moment, then shook her head.

No, it's fine. Nothing I did was remotely shovel. I just "buried" some characters with my shovel. That's all. That's...

"What the hell do I mean, 'that's all'?!" exclaimed Catria.

"Ah, she noticed, shovel!" giggled Lithisia.

Unbeknownst to her, Catria's built-up Madness

Resistance had already burst past Shovel Level 10. She shook off the burden of epiphany and declared, "The Water Tower! Let's hurry to the Water Tower, Lucy!"

"Yes, Great Hero Catria!"

And so our heroes made their way to their next objective with their hopeful angel in tow.

"Water, eh? Perfect. I can just see it," Alan whispered to himself.

Lucy's cultivation was speeding up.

PART 34
The Lady Knight Defeats the Sky Mage King

THE PARTY MADE FAST WORK of the Water Tower. While they stormed it, Lucy acquired a new skill with the help of Alan's wise direction. It allowed Lucy to fill the Holy Grail of Water at the top of the Tower with holy water.

The group was now in the Tower garden, sorting through their information to determine their next move.

"Squall Magic." Lucy gazed at the name of her new skill and sighed. "Ah, I did it. Great Hero Catria, I acquired a reasonable skill!"

"Indeed you have. I'm happy for you, Lucy."

Lucy was as delighted as a little kid on Christmas. Catria didn't want to destroy her smile, so she hid the fact that the actual spelling of the skill was "Scooall Magic." Catria was a kindhearted Holy Knight.

Ring a ding ding!

This sound meant Lucy's status had updated yet again. Her new title was: "Angel of the Five Great Elements."

Lucy's eyes sparkled as she clapped her hands together. "I-I can't believe it! I've become an Angel of the Elements...!"

"What's that mean?"

"It's a title given to only the most elite of angels, those who are capable of manipulating the four great elements: earth, water, wind, and fire!"

"I see... Wait, four elements?"

But the title was "Angel of the *Five* Great Elements."

Uh oh.

A chill ran down Catria's spine. Why? Because Lithisia was giggling. The fifth element probably had something to do with shovels.

"Hee hee hee." Lithisia tapped her smiling lips with her shovel. "An Angel of the Elements..."

But Lucy seemed pleased as punch, so Catria opted to steer the conversation in safer direction, though she did pause to consider... Perhaps it'd be better for humanity if they left the princess in this floating city?

"Whatever..." Catria shook her head. "Alan, let's hurry forward."

In any event, they had acquired all of the Elemental Keys. It was time to head for the central tower, which was larger than all the other four combined. If anything, it was more like a fortress. A true relic, these were ruins from the ancient magic kingdom. However, the tower rumbled even now and was clearly still active with some kind of dormant force.

According to Lucy, the Golden Orb was in the treasure vault of this tower.

"There are magic traps, so be careful, Catria," said Alan.

"Can't you just bury them?"

"I can, but this is a chance for you and Lucy to grow and learn. You two are going to do the digging."

"I refuse."

The back-sass continued as they at last opened the tower gate with the four Elemental Keys, which was made from the same kind of mysterious black material that decorated all Rahzelfo. A single path led forward, eventually coming to an open hall illuminated by pale magical lights. It was a throne room, decked with all manner of glittering jewels. Perhaps due to an enchantment, the room showed no sign of age or deterioration. It was also completely empty.

The party searched everywhere, but aside from the entrance, there were no other doors.

"This is where the treasure vault should be..." said Lucy.

"There's probably a hidden passageway somewhere. Catria, try to dig it up," said Alan.

"I told you, I refuse!"

An unfamiliar voice responded to Catria's angry shout, echoing through the throne room. "How rude. Who dares disturb my slumber?"

"Is someone there?!"

The voice in question sounded like it belonged to a serious but youthful woman. Once Catria realized this, a dark aura enveloped the throne like a tornado of shadows. Although they were indoors, lightning crackled.

Suddenly, sitting on the once empty throne was a raven-haired woman clad in an elegant black dress. She looked to be around twenty years old. Within her narrow eyes resided a ghastly power.

"Who are you?!" gasped Catria.

The woman chuckled. "Hm. You know not the face of the Mage King, Farshinal? Barbarians, the lot of you."

Farshinal... Catria recognized the name. The 88th Mage King, the Sky Queen, said to be the cruelest and most beautiful of all mortals.

In order, Farshinal pointed her finger at Catria, Alan, and Lithisia. "Mmm, three barbarians..."

Her expression turned serious as her gaze landed on the last member of their party. Lucy shivered.

"And one of the gods' little wax dolls. How uninspired."

"?!"

"My world needs not the hand of any god. Your presence insults me. Die."

Farshinal made an arcane gesture and a charged wave of darkness took shape in her palm. It formed into a spear and fired at the flick of her wrist, careening toward Lucy at unbearable speed. If she didn't dodge it...

No, it was too late. It was a homing spear! Maybe Lucy could counter with a Holy Lance? No, it was all too late!

Gabriella, I'm sorry!

"JUSTICE STREAM!"

KA-CHOOOOOOOOOM!

"Huh...?"

"Lucy! Snap out of it! Don't let her intimidate you! She's our enemy!"

Catria had responded near instantaneously and countered the dark energy with her (self-proclaimed) Justice Stream.

"Alan, we're going in!"

Alan glanced at Catria, then Lucy, then Lithisia. He bowed his head, thinking it over. "Nah. I'm leaving you in charge this time, Catria. I'm going to go get Alice."

"Excuse me?!"

What the hell was he saying?!

"When it comes to Mage Kings, undead are the way to go. We'll have Alice place Farshinal under her control, then we can get some info out of her."

"No, wait! Hold up! Are you going to make the two of us buy you time?!"

"Didn't I tell you I wanted to make this run about the two of you?"

That was ridiculous! Catria's gaze darted back toward Farshinal, who was once again collecting arcane energy into her hand. Quite frankly, Catria had been lucky when she countered that last attack. She wasn't confident she could pull it off a second time.

But despite the protest in Catria's eyes, Alan merely shook his head. "No, you're not buying me time. You're going to beat the living hell out of the Mage King."

"Wha?!"

"Believe in yourself, Catria. As far as I can tell..." Alan grinned and stabbed his shovel into the ground. He then patted her on the shoulder. "Between you, Lithisia, and Lucy, she doesn't stand a chance."

"Wha?"

"And if the going gets real tough and things look dicey, just yell out 'shove, shove, shovel!' and I'll come running."

"You really think I'd be able to yell that nonsense if I was in trouble?!"

"Catria. You're never going to grow as a Holy Knight if you keep relying on others."

"Urgh!"

Alan smiled gently. "Don't rely on my shovel. Scoop others from danger as a Holy Knight."

With that, Alan vanished.

Catria gripped her blade. Her pride and honor as a Holy Knight. Could she really do this without Alan?

"I undershovelstand, Sir Miner!" Meanwhile, Lithisia was getting pumped.

More importantly, would Catria really be able to work with this crazy princess to beat the Sky Queen?!

"Hm, he fled, eh? A wise barbarian. I'll save him for last."

Farshinal cackled, overcome with glee. She clearly felt she had already won. Truth be told, she possessed a daunting magical strength. She was at least on par with the true form of the Hydra the party had fought in the Lactia Republic. She might well be stronger. Even worse, Alan was gone.

Would Catria really be able to do battle with the Mage King?

"Great Hero Catria..." Lucy whispered from off to the side, her voice weak. The immense pressure rolling off of the Sky Queen had nearly robbed her of her will to fight.

In that case... Catria unsheathed her sword. "Don't worry, Lucy."

This wasn't about whether she could win or not. It was about the person next to her, depending on her.

In that case, she had to do this. Just like Alan always had.

"YAAAAAAAAAAAH!"

Catria gripped her Holy Knight Blade and yelled as loudly as she could. A light blue aura erupted from her body. One move. She'd pour all of her spiritual energy into one fatal strike and decimate the Mage King.

Farshinal laughed merrily. "Impressive spiritual power, to say the least. Let me start with cutting it down. Forbidden Spell, Mind Hurricane!"

The Mage King snapped her fingers and three magic-enhancing orbs whooshed into the throne room. All at once the nightmarish cries of a wraith filled the air, and it felt as though the fierce storm could blow away their very thoughts.

This was bad. Catria had to hold onto herself. "This can't stop...me... YAAAAAAAAH!"

Compared to the princess's Shovel Mind Control, this was nothing. Catria shook her head, ridding herself of the awful sounds echoing in her skull.

"Hm, you possess Spiritual Resistance, do you? How rare. But what about the angel?"

"Ah...AGHHH!!!"

Lucy fell to her knees. She might have Madness Resistance, but she couldn't withstand this terrible onslaught. Catria had to save her, but how?!

"ALAN! SCOOP! ALAN!"

Someone started to yell; it was Lithisia.

The princess held out her shovel and chanted in simple repetition, but her earnest cry erased the devastating howl of the Mind Hurricane.

"Scoop! Alan! Scoop! Alan!"

Lithisia never raised her voice, but for some reason, the shrieks of the wraiths were driven completely from her party's minds. Soon, her chants filled the room entirely. As they did, Farshinal's floating orbs of magic changed shape, morphing into the form of shovels.

"Stop it! Scoop that song! No more! ALAN! Wait, what am I saying, shovel?!" Farshinal gripped her head as Lithisia continued to chant.

Incredible. The Mage King's spiritual magic was receding back into her!

"Nooo! Scoop! Scoop the shoveling scooper dig dig AAAAHHHHH!!!!" wailed Lucy.

Oh, and Lucy was also being affected by Lithisia's chanting.

"Your Highness! Stop singing! Lucy's shovelizing!" cried Catria.

"But this is our chance, shovel! ALAN! SCOOP!"

"Your Highness?!"

Crap, crap, crap! Someone stop her before the whole world is enveloped in shovels! Catria thought desperately.

"SHOVELING SCOOOOOOP! OOOOOOOH! W-Wave Motion of Darkness, scooooop!" Farshinal fired dark energy from the tips of her fingers and the orbs in the throne room cracked like glass. Their remaining magical energy poured out onto the black floor and melted away.

Finally, Lithisia's "Alan Wave" subsided.

"Haaah, haaah, haaah..." Lucy was drenched in sweat and tears.

Meanwhile, the Mage King had collapsed over her throne. "Grah... Who are you?! How could you reverse my magic?!"

"Ah, the orbs are gone, shovel..." sighed Lithisia. "That was such a perfect shovel chance..."

Catria was shaken to the bone. Princess Lithisia was horrifying.

"Haaah, haaah. Great Hero Catria, stay by my side. Get the shovels away from me!"

"Don't worry, Lucy! I'm here. I'm here! You're safe!"

"Y-you're incredible, Great Hero Catria... You were able to withstand that awful, awful voice..."

Catria was rendered speechless. *Wait, she's right. Why didn't the princess's chant have an effect on me? No...it's probably because I'm dealing with her all day every day, yeah, that's gotta be it.*

"A-anyway, the Mage King is weak now! This is our chance!"

Catria swung her Holy Knight Blade and advanced on the Mage King Farshinal. Catria channeled all the power in her body into her sword, into the idea she wanted to "Save the world."

Holy light grew within and flowed out of her. She had to defeat this thing here and now. If she didn't, the world would be destroyed...primarily by Princess Lithisia!

"JUSTICE...STREAM!!!"

Catria released her Justice Stream at full power.

"A BARBARIAN LIKE YOU COULD NEVER BEAT MEEEEEEEE!"

Farshinal heaved herself up from her throne in a rage and threw both her hands toward Catria, firing a counter-wave of dark energy. The two beams collided head-on, shaking the very atmosphere of the throne room.

"Nrgh...aaaah!"

Inch by inch, Catria was pushed back. The Mage King was indeed strong.

Who was it again that had the nerve to say this'd be easy?

Alan! Curse you! Should I just yell "shove, shove, shovel!" and get this over with?

But a voice came to Catria in her moment of weakness.

"Catria! Let me help you with my Holy Lanse!"

Lucy placed her hand on Catria's where she held her sword. The white energy of Catria's light grew somehow purer, larger. Bright and strong enough to combat Farshinal!

"An angel?! An angel dares to try and stop me?!" Farshinal's dark energy grew as if in spite and rage.

Just as their collision of power appeared to draw equal, Lithisia dove in and offered up her red shovel in service to the cause.

"ALAN! ALAN!"

The once destroyed magic orbs regained their form. They circled up from the floor, making "scoop, scoop" sounds as their magical power rebooted.

"What?! That's impossible! You're reusing my magical power?!"

"Your mistake was not absorbing their remnant energies when you left them lying about on the floor." Lithisia grinned devilishly. "Digging up buried magical power and reusing it...that's the miner way!"

"Stop it! Stop at once! Don't denigrate my magic with your shovel!"

Once again, chants of "ALAN" rang out in every corner of the vast room.

This is bad! This is real bad! I have to stop her! I'm the only one who can! And I made a vow! I promised myself I'd never lose to Alan or Princess Lithisia!

I'm going to save this world (from the corruption of the shovel)!

"AAAAAAAAAAAHHHH!!!"
The moment Catria recalled her vow, her Justice Stream billowed. Holy energy rushed like a torrent, completely enveloping the Mage King's dark energy. It was enough to blow away not only the Mage King Farshinal but the entire throne itself.

"Aaaaaaaaaarrrghh!"
As soon as Farshinal passed out on the floor, the orbs vanished.

Lithisia dropped her shoulders in disappointment. "Aw, Catria... Next time don't rush like that."

Catria couldn't reply. She rested her sword on the ground, breathing heavily. Somehow, she managed to gather enough strength to turn toward the princess. "Your Highness..."

"Whavel is it?"

"I will never...lose to...the shovel..." Having said her piece, Catria collapsed to the floor, exhausted.

Lithisia knelt and lovingly cradled her friend's body.

"Catria...my dear friend...that desire of yours to pierce the laws of this world..." She smiled. "Is already oh-so-shoveltastic."

"You're...wrong..."

"So stubborn, shovel."

Catria lost consciousness. This was how she took her first step toward becoming a real Holy Knight.

A few minutes later, Catria woke to find her wounds treated. Alan had returned, along with Alice.

"How was it, Catria?" Alan asked as he helped her up. "A cinch, right?"

"Hmph. Mostly because of Princess Lithisia."

The battle hadn't been a "cinch," but neither had it been some hard-fought victory. It was something far more horrific. For now, Catria was happy Princess Lithisia was her ally...but was she really? No matter how many times Catria went over it in her head, the princess seemed a hundred times more terrible and sublime than the Mage King.

"Alice, what's the deal with Farshinal?" asked Alan.

"Uugh… I'm not some undead handywoman, you know." Nevertheless, Alice placed her hand on Farshinal's head and pressed her fingers as if she were playing the piano.

Under Alice's touch, the Mage King drooled and twitched.

"Well, I've placed her under my control. We're lucky she's completely drained of magical power."

"I want to ask her about the whereabouts of the Golden Orb, and any memories she might have of Pazuzu."

"Hrm, wait…wait… Is this it?"

"Ah, aaahhh…Pazuzu…the orb…Pazu…" Farshinal's eyes shot open. "Initiate Protection Program."

Farshinal's body glowed red with deadly astral energy.

Alice rapidly backpedaled. "Eeek! It's a trap! Everyone get back!"

"DIG!"

Alan immediately pierced Farshinal's body with his shovel, and just as he did, the red glow vanished. He had buried the trap.

While this horror nearly befell them, Lithisia and Catria were munching on shookies (Lithisia's special cookies) without a care in the world.

Alice's mouth hung wide open.

"It looks like we've stumbled upon something important, Alice. Please continue."

Alan seemed totally at ease. Alice sighed deeply. *In the time I've been away, they've gotten even weirder.*

PART 35

The Miner Blasts the Floating City with the Wave Motion Shovel Blast

THE PARTY surrounded the astral beauty Farshinal in her conquered throne room. From the info Alice had extracted from her, they now knew the plan to reopen Hell's Gate was in fact a feint. Pazuzu's true aim was to capture a greater angel and use them as a sacrifice for the "Angel Fall" ceremony. In other words, their enemy's objective was Gabriella.

For her part, Farshinal was nothing more than an underling resurrected by Pazuzu's power.

"Whew, in that case, we have no need to worry!" said Lucy.

"Lucy, when it comes to safety first, one must never let their guard down."

If Gabriella were to flee back to Heaven, this whole thing would collapse on itself. But the greater demons weren't stupid. They surely had a Plan B.

"I agree with Alan," said Catria. "Especially that one mustn't ever let their guard down around him."

"Really?"

"*Really*."

The moment anyone let their guard down around Alan, their sanity was in terrible danger. Catria made sure to impress this point on Lucy.

"So what do we do with this woman?" asked Alice. "I could always absorb her."

"I have a shovelingly great idea. Please connect us to the shovel prison in the World Tree Castle." Lithisia giggled.

What exactly was this princess thinking of doing with the Mage King? Well, she was probably going to shovel her.

"So they want to sacrifice a greater angel...?" Lucy murmured.

"Lucy, does that ring a bell at all?"

"N-no, of course not." Lucy shook her head, causing her pink hair to wave through the air and her breasts to bounce lightly. "I'm probably just overthinking it. There's no way something like that could exist in the world below."

"Lucy, I suggest not hiding anything from Alan," said Catria.

"Huh?"

But Alan was already digging through the space above Lucy's head with his shovel. "I see...an Angel Furnace. It's a magic tool that absorbs an angel's very existence and outputs its energy."

"What the?! Wh-what did you just do?!"

"I unearthed the deeper meaning in your words."

"Don't do that without my permission!" Lucy snapped, her cheeks red.

It was indeed awful of him to do that without her permission, but even Lucy was unsure of what exactly was awful about his shoveling otherwise. Either way, if he was going to dig into her, she'd have liked for him to ask for her consent first. Not that she'd say yes to any such vile thing!

Lucy shoved past this strange internal conflict of hers. "A-anyway, that was awful of you, Miner Alan!"

She did her best to shoot him a glare while underlining that what he did was no good at all.

"Hm, how odd." Catria found she had questions about the angel's glare.

Lucy's anger toward Alan for shovelizing Gabriella was clearly thinning. She still didn't like him much, but it wasn't like she hated him from the bottom of her heart.

Or at least, that was what it felt like. But why? Was she that happy her angelic rank had improved?

"Hee hee, the effects of ALAN from our battle with Farshinal have begun to surface, shovel," said Lithisia.

Catria decided to buy some good earplugs when they returned to the surface world. It was getting more and more dangerous to listen to this princess's words.

After digging through Rahzelfo for a bit, the party came upon the treasure vault of the ancient magic kingdom. It honestly seemed more like a prison than anything else.

The walls and floor shone black, made from the same mysterious material as the gate to the central tower. A magic circle was inscribed on the floor in dark red blood. However, hovering above the center of the circle wasn't the Golden Orb, but a larger, egg-shaped object.

On occasion, a ripple ran through the object. Multiple tentacles stretched from it, squirming through the air in search of some unknown aim. The mere sight of this grotesque thing was enough to make a person want to vomit.

"An Angel Furnace...?!" Lucy's voice shuddered with fear as she backed away from the tentacles. "It's been activated... Multiple angels have already been dissolved within it!"

"This egg used to be an angel or something?"

Lucy nodded, on the verge of tears.

An Angel Furnace, huh? This was Alan's first time seeing this particular magic tool. Indeed, he could sense the holy essence of angels trapped within it, as well as an immense amount of energy. It at least rivaled the destructive power of the King of Hell, the "Demogorgon," and its Netherball attack.

The Angel Furnace was ready for activation even without the addition of Gabriella. Alan had to do something fast, so he whipped out his shovel.

"Wait, Miner Alan! If you destroy it, it'll go out of control and..."

"Got it. Back away, Lucy. I'll handle this."

"Oh no, I don't believe you will."

A hoarse voice rang out and ZAP! Black lightning crackled along the surface of the Angel Furnace and the entire underground vault began to quake. Alan gripped his shovel, shifting into a guard stance.

As he did, a winged demon manifested overhead and descended before the party. Slightly taller than Alan, its wicked horns and vast leathery wings were what really sold its appearance. The evil light in its eyes was far more intense than any demon Alan had encountered outside the very depths of Hell.

The shaking grew more violent.

"Hee hee, Zeleburg has failed, has he?" said the demon. "To think beings of the surface world would make it to the floating city of Rahzelfo."

Lucy shot the vile creature an enraged glare. *How many angels has this monster killed?! It can't get away with this!*

"Great Hero Catria, Miner Alan, this is Pazuzu!" Lucy shouted. "Please, lend me your strength and..."

But before Lucy could finish speaking, Alan shot his Rapid Fire Wave Motion Shovel Blast.

"DIG!"

KA-CHOOOOOOOOM!

It blew Pazuzu away, along with the wall of the treasure vault. Sword in hand, Lucy was frozen in place.

Huh? It's over? Before I could even ask for help?!

Catria patted Lucy on the shoulder. "Remember, Lucy. Never let your guard down around Alan."

"Huh...?"

"By the time you get fired up, chances are pretty good he's already done his thing." Catria stared blankly into the distance. She knew trying to explain was futile, but even still.

"Huh? Er, wha?!" Lucy blinked rapidly in an attempt

to understand what had just transpired. *Um, the evil Demon King is certainly gone...or appears to be gone? But...*

The quaking of the ground grew ever more violent and the Angel Furnace continued to crackle even more fiercely. Something was happening, but what?

Lithisia looked down at a shovel-shaped thing in her hands. "Sir Miner, according to my Shovepass, our altitude is dropping."

"I can feel it as well. I knew it... We don't have time."

"Er, Miner Alan? What do you mean?" Lucy asked.

"The floating city is currently falling to the surface."

No, that can't be! Lucy frantically looked out of the hole Alan had opened in the wall. Outside, a vicious gale blew in an upward direction. Also, they were accelerating. If this gargantuan city-continent were to collide with the surface world, a continent-sized hole would be blown off of the planet.

The speed of their descent likely had something to do with the Angel Furnace. They were just getting faster!

I will never forgive them for using angel power like this! Lucy thought. *There has to be a way to stop our fall!*

As if in response to her thoughts, Alan took up his shovel.

"N-no, Alan! You can't! You mustn't destroy it! Its amassed energy will go berserk!" Lucy flailed her hands at the miner. *This is bad! I'm the only one who knows anything about the Angel Furnace!*

"I'm not really out to destroy it..."

"But if we're going to stop our fall, we have to get control of..." Lucy stopped.

In her training, she had been taught how to control an Angel Furnace. It was a terrible technique, but this horrible, awful thing, was their only chance. Lucy hugged her shivering body.

It'll be okay. I'm the little sister of Gabriella, an archangel. It's scary... It's terrifying, but...

"Lucy, we're getting out of here. Let's..."

Lucy heard Catria's voice. A true Holy Knight who, despite being a human, could wield the Holy Blade.

This true hero saved me (from shovel corruption) so many times. I have no reason not to sacrifice my life for her.

"No, that won't be necessary." Lucy stood tall, doing her best to hold back her tears. She seized one of the thrashing tentacles connected to the Angel Furnace and stuck it directly to her own bountiful chest.

GRIIIIIND.

It immediately began to devour her heart.

"Urrrrraggggggh!"

"W-wait, what are you doing?!" Catria dashed over to her.

"Alan...Miner Alan...use the Ring of the Archangel... Give me my orders!"

"What?"

"If you command me...to get inside of the Angel Furnace...I can control...agh!" The tentacle sucked at Lucy's essence. Her chest burned hot, as did her mind. Her entire body was being absorbed. *No! I'm not going to hold out long...but I have to!*

Catria tried to wrench the tentacle off Lucy, but to no avail. It was now a part of her. Every time it convulsed, an eldritch jolt ran through Lucy's body.

"Ngaah...AAAAAAAHHHHH!"

The foreign object pushed into her, but she couldn't resist it. She had to let it in. The only way to control the Angel Furnace was to become a part of it. She would lose consciousness, but a ringbearer could still force her to take action according to their will.

"Damnit! What is with this thing?! Lucy, stop it! Stop this stupidity at once!"

"Aaaggghhh...Great Hero Catria...it's okay... If I can use this...life to save you... AAAAHHH!!!"

"You don't have to throw your life away! We can still be saved!"

"Huh?"

"We can. For sure. Like, it's not even a big deal."

Finally, Alan stepped in. "Perfect. Preparations complete. We're all getting out of here."

Alan scooped up Lucy and the Angel Furnace with one hand (transportation was a miner's specialty), then exited from the hole he had created when he annihilated Pazuzu into the rushing wind. Aboard his Shovel Glider, the entire party fled Rahzelfo.

They shot into the sky, buffeted by powerful gusts, but soon they were gliding easily down to the surface. Once on solid ground, they realized to their horror that the floating city was on a collision course with the fields of Rostir, plummeting like an incoming comet.

If it were to make contact with the earth, it would turn the entire nation of Rostir into one big old crater.

Alan had only one option.

"DIG!"

KA-CHOOOOOOOOOM!

The beam of light he fired from the land below pierced the sky itself, almost like a reverse-flowing comet. It was Alan's Hyper-Wide Wave Motion Shovel Blast.

Alan fired the hyper-wide beam at about 20 percent of its normal power, but it was more than enough to engulf and evaporate Rahzelfo. Just like that, Farshinal's arcane lair and the pride of the ancient magic kingdom was as nothing. If mages seeking the knowledge of old were to bear witness to this moment, they would undoubtedly burst into tears, but all of that was kind of beside the point.

This all wrapped up in the twenty seconds after Lucy let herself get caught by the Angel Furnace.

"Um, what?" The tentacle attached to Lucy's chest wriggled as she stared up at the empty sky, her existence continuing to be slowly absorbed by the Angel Furnace. *Um, where's Rahzelfo? I was supposed to use my life to stop it from falling.*

"Didn't I tell you we'd be okay, Lucy?" said Catria.

"Um, but, er... Whaaaa?!"

"Now then, how do we get this thing off of you...? Whoa! It's fusing with you!"

It was too late. Lucy was a part of the Angel Furnace. *No, wait, come on! Really?! After all of this?!*

As Lucy pleaded within her fading consciousness, a hoarse voice rang out from above.

"How dare you... That light... Do you possess a Heavenly Artifact?!"

There in the sky was Pazuzu, who had supposedly been blown away by Alan. However, the demon's appearance was...wrong. For one, it was many multiple times larger than its original appearance in the floating city. For another, it roared as it circled the skies in an enormous draconic body.

Alan peered up and observed its movements with a careful eye. "Huh, so the thing from before was just a splinter, then? I'm assuming this one's the real deal."

Most great demons had some sort of resistance to death. As such, even if you beat one of its splinters, the main body would remain unharmed.

"Haaah, haaah... In that case...!" Lucy managed to raise her voice despite the ongoing diminishment of her entire being. *I'm going to be useful this time! I'm going to defeat the demon... I'm going to help!*

Lucy did her best to suppress the quivering of her body as she stood before Alan.

"Don't worry... With the power of the Angel Furnace, I can, urgh, seal its resistance to death...argh...!"

Lucy would use the furnace's pent-up power to defeat the demon and save Catria once and for all. For the second time in one minute, she steeled her resolve.

I have no reason not to sacrifice my life for her, right?

"Lucy."

"Miner Alan, aaaagggghhhh!!! Command...me...!"

Alan frowned at Lucy as she pleaded with him, her face covered in tears. "Stand aside," he said.

"Huh?"

Alan wrote the words "Pazuzu's Death Resistance" into the ground and buried it. Boom. Resistance sealed.

He then fired off his Hyper-Wide Wave Motion Shovel Blast again, this time at 50 percent maximum strength.

KA-CHOOOOM!

This half-measure was more than enough to engulf Pazuzu's entire body in light and vanquish him forever. The second reverse comet of the day.

"..."

The Angel Furnace tentacle absorbed the last dregs of Lucy's existence. She was now mostly transparent. As her consciousness disappeared within the white egg of the purified Angel Furnace, she remembered Catria's words: "You must never let your guard down around Alan."

Tears poured from Lucy's eyes. *Why...why did I not listen to her?*

The last thing she remembered was Gabriella's face during the final fleeting moments of her sanity.

"I truly am blessed...I get to die as an angel..."

Yes... Lucy smiled through her tears. *In that case, I too am fortunate...*

She had constantly let her guard down. She was a fool, an idiot, even. But at least she'd get to leave this world without being further corrupted by the shovel.

➤

Ten seconds later on the fields of Rostir, Alan held the Golden Orb, which had fallen from Pazuzu's enormous body.

"Welp. Now that we've finished off Pazuzu and have the orb, let's save Lucy from the Angel Furnace," Alan said.

"Here it comes! Sir Miner's classic Angel Scoop! Time to go retrieve an angel from certain doom, shovel!"

"You make it sound like he's scooping up goldfish or something..." Alice said.

"I knew it. So you can save her?" Catria asked.

Alan remained completely unfazed as Lucy vanished, so Catria figured as much.

"At the end of the day, it's a furnace, just like a blast furnace. This means you can scoop up its insides with a shovel."

"Please don't do that to a poor blast furnace."

Catria was well aware her sentence made no sense. Well, whatever, it was impossible to measure this man's shovel with common sense or real world knowledge.

"Think about it this way. Melting in a furnace is a good experience for angels."

"H-how so? I feel so bad for Lucy..."

Catria did feel bad, but she also knew this was their best course of action. She looked up at the empty blue sky as it crept toward night. For a moment, she saw the smiling face of Lucy among the glittering stars.

Lucy, I know you think you've gone to the next life, but... unfortunately for you, the true shovel corruption is about to begin.

PART 36

Lucy's Soft and Melty Shovel

ALAN BURIED HIS SHOVEL into the Angel Furnace and mentally dove deep within. This was the one way he could save Lucy and the other angels who had been absorbed by the magic tool. He closed his eyes and dug his shovel into the device again and again; it felt a lot like cracking a succession of eggshells. At last, he met no more resistance and opened his eyes.

Alan was met with a wash of white steam.

"A bath...?"

In front of him was a curtain with the words "Angel Bath" written on it. Alan glanced inside and found not Lucy but a different angel sitting on her knees on the watcher's seat with a peaceful little smile. Even though she had a towel wrapped around her body, she was pretty much naked. Through the thick steam, her plump chest and thighs were just visible.

This was the interior of the Angel Furnace.

Who's the idiot that made this thing? Alan thought.

When the angel noticed him, her smile widened. "Welcome to the Angel Furnace, sir."

Her tone was something like that of a newlywed wife.

"You're the supervisor, I take it?" said Alan. "Or should I say, the Angel Furnace in and of itself?"

"Correct. I can tell you're not an angel...but I suppose that's not a problem." The angel on the watcher's seat took out a wash basin with the word "Angel" written on it. Inside of it was "melting soap," "soft soap," and "heavenly rinse." This was clearly a set of liquids for bathing.

"No towel?"

"Oh my. You won't be needing one. I'm sure you already realize that." The Angel giggled, her eyes glistening mischievously. "All angels melt into me. There is no leaving the bath."

It appeared the bath-like setting was the only joke here. It was time to save Lucy.

Alan buried the evil watcher-angel in the image of a snowy mountain, causing her to cry out in shock. He then entered the changing room but nobody was there. However, a significant quantity of angel clothes and underwear were neatly folded and placed in baskets. A sweet feminine scent lingered in the air.

Also, though he hadn't yet noticed, Alan had been reduced to his nude form with only a towel slung around his waist. The laws of physics weren't something the furnace particularly cared about.

Moving on, Alan slid open a steamed-up glass door. "Hrm."

A blast of warm air hit his body, accompanied by the lilting sound of women chatting.

Spread before Alan was Heaven. Or was it Hell? In every corner of the stone bath were angels; about one hundred in total. They were lounging in the water, enjoying themselves with expressions of pure joy... Perhaps it was more accurate to describe it as something like a trance-like state? After all, their wings were melting.

In a corner of the bath, one angel still had the shine of reason in her eyes. She was surrounded by five other angels, who were washing her. The angels cleaned her long, shining hair, intertwined their fingers with hers, and pressed their chests up against her own. With each move they made, a little more life left the lone angel's eyes. As this happened, soapsuds bubbled on the surface of the water around her.

"Oh, my...a new friend. And so muscular, too...!"

As Alan evaluated the unfolding scene, multiple angels approached him. They all appeared to be in the prime of life, and the gazes they shot him were nothing if not suggestive as their breasts heaved. Their eyes spoke to him as they reached out with their hands.

Melt together with us... Let us intertwine in this Angel Bath... It'll feel, so, so good. Even better than going to Heaven...

Alan frowned at these angels and scooped them up with the metal head of his shovel.

"DIG!"

"EEEEEK!"

One by one, the naked angels were tossed into the changing room. They landed head-first into the bath towels Alan had prepared there.

"Hey! Who do you think you are, human?!"

"Don't you want to melt away in this beautiful Angel Bath?!"

"I don't care if you're an angel or a bagel," said Alan.

Shoop, shoop!

Alan scooped the remaining two angels into the changing room.

"I have no interest in women who lack depth in their hearts—women with no room for digging."

Alan was a man with a healthy interest in women,

but he felt zero attraction to a woman whose heart had melted into the Angel Furnace. In that sense, sharing a bath at the World Tree Castle with Fio had been treacherous indeed. If not for Alan's adamantine levels of self-control, he might have been incapable of pulling himself away from her.

It wasn't a question of her figure. Yes, she was a lovely girl, but! Deep within Fio's coy form lay a pure desire to rebuild elven civilization. That depth was what attracted Alan. It made him want to dig into Fio's heart.

Of course, she was his precious niece (if unrelated by blood), so he'd never lay a finger on her.

In any case, it was time to scoop up the rest of these angels and destroy the furnace.

Alan splashed through the bath, scooping angels into the changing room as he went along and calling out for Lucy. Finally, he found the face he was looking for. Lucy was squished between two angels who were washing her wings with their hands.

Lucy shook with each scrub. She appeared to be in a trance. "Aahh... Pheeew..."

"What beautiful wings...so soft, so fluffy."

"Let us melt together! Melty, melty, puffy, puffy..."

"Outta the way," said Alan.

"EEEEK!"

Scoop, scoop!

In an instant, Alan launched the two angels into the changing room.

"Lucy, it's me. Alan."

"Ah...Alan...?" Lucy stared at the man with droopy eyes. "Who...Alan?"

"Hrm."

"More importantly...I want to melt... More puffy, puff... Let me melt..." Lucy had lost her memories and her body was going limp. Her plentiful breasts jiggled slightly as she wrapped her arms over them. She tentatively brought her wings around Alan's back and caressed him. *I want to melt. I want to be melted. I want to become soft...*

"All right, I'm going to save you now, Lucy." Alan completely ignored her and took up his shovel. There was no world in which Alan would fall to these inviting pleas, not when Lucy had lost her heart. *It's about time to unearth her memories.*

"Please shovel wait, Sir Alan!"

When Alan turned to the voice, he found a black-haired angel. It was Gabriella. Unlike the other angels, she had a bath towel wrapped around her. That being said, it was only a single bath towel, and it did little to hide her voluptuous body line. However, also unlike the other angels, her eyes retained their sanity.

"Eh, Gabriella? What are you doing here?"

"I got a Shovel Call from Princess Lithisia. She told me my little sister's heart and body had been absorbed by the Angel Furnace."

"But how did you get in here?"

"I asked Lady Catria to help. She managed to get me in with her shovel."

Alan nodded in approval. The lady knight was inching ever closer to becoming a proper shovel wielder.

"Lucy's going to be fine," Alan assured Gabriella as she splashed over to him. "I was just about to unearth her heart."

"Please let me help, shovel. I beg of you!"

"Help...?"

"I'm her older sister. With me here, it should be possible to unearth Lucy's memories."

"Well..." Truth be told, Alan could scoop up Lucy's melted memories by himself, though it would in fact be easier to find them with Gabriella present. More importantly, he didn't want to be dismissive of her desire to save her little sister.

Alan nodded, and Gabriella embraced Lucy from behind. The two angels, their skin warm and flush from the bath, slowly turned to face the miner.

"Sir Alan, I'm ready... Your shovel, please."

The angel sisters held each other and looked at Alan.

We'll accept everything you have together.

Or at least, that's what it felt like they were saying.

But Alan needed to focus. He aimed his shovel at the two angels where they were partially submerged in the bath and struck the water in a straight line.

SHEEEEN!

A burst of steam shot into the air, revealing a video projection. In the video, two young angels ran around a shrine.

"Ah...uhh...?"

"Lucy, try to remember. Think about our time together..."

Lucy showed faint signs of responding to Gabriella's voice. *My head feels empty... Who am I? I don't know... But somebody's holding me. What a familiar feeling...a familiar scent...? I...I know who this is.*

"Come now, Lucy. Look."

The projection in front of them showed a sight she knew.

"Gabriella! Today I'm gonna become an angel!"

"Well said, my beloved little sister."

I know this... After this, I received my blessing from the head deity of our Pantheon. My angel wings...my halo...

The video feed distorted.

"Angel Lucy. As proof of your status as a servant of the heavens..."

The shine of life began to return to Lucy's eyes. *That's right... After this, I received proof of my status, proof of my angel-hood, from the head deity...*

"I bestow upon you the Angelic Shovel."

CRAAAACK.

The sound of glass shattering could be heard from the changing room.

The glimmer of life had returned to Lucy's eyes, but so had confusion.

"W-wait, something's off about this..."

A shovel? Did I really receive a shovel? Seriously? Are these really my memories?

"My word! Lucy, are your memories coming back?!"

"I-I think so, but something seems...off."

"We have to keep going! Sir Alan! Ready the next scoop!"

Alan silently thrust his shovel into the hot water again, causing the video feed to change. This time, it showed a vast field beneath the brightly shining sun. As a member of the heavenly army and an angel-soldier trainee, Lucy was participating in her first real battle. Up until then, she'd only watched Gabriella in combat.

"Lucy, watch me carefully." Gabriella smiled in front of the injured Lucy.

Ah! I remember now! Gabriella's special attack, the...

"HOLY WAVE MOTION SHOVEL BLAST!"

KA-CHOOOOOOOOM!

The Gabriella in the video held a shovel in her hands and fired off a Wave Motion Shovel Blast. All the other angels on the battlefield were holding shovels as well. Even the demons. Of course they were. Shovels were the strongest weapon in all the realms, heavenly and demonic alike...

"...?"

Wait, what? Had that always been Gabriella's special attack?

"Er, um, dear sister, why do you have a shovel...?"

"A little more, Sir Alan! This is the last scoop!"

Alan once again thrust his shovel forward.

At this, Lucy saw herself searching Rahzelfo, conquering each of the Four Elemental Towers, defeating the Mage King with her shovel, and even trouncing Pazuzu.

"Shovel Angel! Shovel Angel!" All of her friends cheered her on with her new title.

Let us all pay reverence to the Shovel Angel, Lucy! All hail the great Shovel Angel, Lucy! Within the video, humans, angels, and demons alike sang Lucy's praises.

"Ah... Shovel...Shovel Angel...?!"

Gabriella embraced her sister tightly and whispered into her ears. "That's right... You're a Shovel Angel... No, you're the Shovel Archangel, Lucy."

"Shovel...Archangel...? I am...? Foolish old me?!"

Lucy could feel herself getting excited. She was filled with joy. Now she was on the same level as her beloved sister. Despite thinking herself a failure, she was now an archangel like Gabriella. Everything would be fine. She had some doubts about the integrity of her memories, but that had to be her imagination. She shed tears, but she was certain they were tears of joy.

"Aaahhh... I...the shovel...!" Lucy could feel her memories being filled in with a shovel. "Aaah... Shovel... Archangel...!"

I'm...Lucy. I'm a Shovel Archangel? Is that...really okay? My heart says this is right. My body desires the shovel. Then surely it must be fine! I have no reason to hesitate. All I have to do is empty my heart and accept these memories... Accept the shovel.

The light of the shovel glimmered within Lucy's eyes.

"Wake up, Lucy!"

"?!"

A fierce female voice blew away her tears. "Don't let go of who you are! I'm with you, Lucy!"

The voice was somehow nostalgic.

Wait, that's right. I know this voice.

It was the voice of one who stood against the shovel.

I know this voice!

"Don't you dare lose to the shovel!!!"

Lucy heard the sound of something shattering to pieces. The coffee milk bottle in the changing room had broken.

She stood up in the bath, drenched in sweat and breathing heavily.

This is all wrong. The shovel is wrong. This isn't how my memories are supposed to be. Right, Catria?!

"This is...WRONG!" Lucy declared as she stood firmly on her own two feet. "I...I'm no Shovel Angel!"

"Ah, she's reverting, shovel! How unfortunate... Let's try one more...eeek!"

THONK.

Gabriella attempted to embrace her little sister once more, but Alan stopped her.

"Gabriella, what did Lithisia put into that head of yours?"

"Ack!"

"One is only truly worth digging into when their heart remains strong. Stop messing around with people's memories."

"I-I'm sorry, shovel."

Lucy was exhausted beyond belief, but life had at last truly returned to her eyes. With great strength, she said, "Miner Alan! I believe it's time we destroy this Angel Furnace!"

"You got that right, but could you cover yourself with a towel first? I can't look at you like this."

"Huh…?" Lucy looked down at her mostly naked body. Her thirty-five inches of breasts. The hot water dripping down her hips. Her tight waist and the small belly button on her stomach. It was all utterly visible.

And then there was her lower body. She wasn't completely naked, and the center of her white garments had an angel wing decoration. Unfortunately, it had been rendered largely translucent in the Angel Bath.

Lucy blazed with utter dismay. "Mm!"

To Alan's surprise, her expression shook his adamantine self-restraint. This experience had given Lucy even greater depths than she earlier possessed.

"EEEEEEEEEEEEK!!!"

"Please cover up."

Lucy hurriedly dropped her body beneath the water.

"Sir Alan, since we're here already, what say the two of us showash your back, shovel?" asked Gabriella.

"No thanks. We're getting out of here, stat."

"Aw, too bad." Gabriella wore a somewhat disappointed expression, one that resembled Lithisia to a tee.

"Great Hero Catria, you have my gratitude. Thank you so very much...!"

The party had scooped up the remaining ninety-nine angels, destroyed the Angel Furnace, and made their way back to the World Tree Castle. Lucy was in the main hall on her knees, bowing to Catria over and over again while expressing her devotion. If not for Catria's words, she would have fallen to the shovel.

"As long as I live and breathe, I vow to serve you, Great Hero Catria!"

"Er, you don't have to go that far, I swear."

Despite her embarrassment, Catria was genuinely happy. Next to her, Lithisia looked disappointed.

"Lithisia... You did something to Gabriella, didn't you?" said Alan.

"Ah, um, no! I just contacted her via Shovel Call is all!" Lithisia's response was all too easy to understand.

"It was almost like you were talking through her body, actually."

"Shovel?!" Lithisia broke out into a cold sweat.

Alan had clearly hit the nail on the head. Lithisia was panicking and clutching her shovel.

Despite his accusation, the miner had trouble believing it. Had this princess really possessed Gabriella's body? Lithisia was crazy, yes, but surely she couldn't be this far gone...

"No, wait," he said. "That's right. Alice and the Mage King."

"Sh-shovel?!" Lithisia was now a waterfall of sweat.

"I-I was against it! Against it, I tell you!" insisted Alice.

Farshinal was capable of advanced spirit magic. Through Alice, Lithisia used Farshinal's power to temporarily transport her spirit into Gabriella's body. As for why, well, she wanted to turn Lucy into a Shovel Angel.

This was bad. Lithisia was mastering the shovel at an absurd rate. Still, there was a part of Alan that was happy someone other than him could master it at all. He wasn't alone in this world. How could someone not be pleased by such a revelation?

"Just don't mess with the soul too much, Lithisia."

"Shorry..."

Alan just couldn't work himself up to be overly strict with her. After all, at the end of the day, nobody had been hurt. Also, the miner's sense of ethics typically sided with the shovel.

"Well, anyway. We've got six orbs now."

On the table in front of the party were all six of the spheres. They only needed one more before they could put an end to Prime Minister Zeleburg's ambitions. As for the location of the final orb, the Purple Orb, Lithisia looked more serious than she ever had.

"It lies in the dark nation, known as the 'Kingdom of Darkness.'"

This was also the location of Zeleburg's base of operations. A stormy region with no sun, it had almost no communication with the outside world. The situation on the ground was completely unknown to anyone who didn't already dwell there. It was also said to be run by demons. Given Zeleburg's rise to power, that was all but certainly the truth.

"The Purple Orb supposedly resides in the underground fortress Mormegil, where the King of Darkness lives."

"An underground fortress, eh? Perfect." Alan smiled his usual smile and held up his shovel. "Shovels are perfect for dealing with the underground."

Amidst the party's confident nods, Catria was still and silent as she thought.

The underground was indeed the perfect place to demonstrate a shovel's power. But seeing how the shovel was already so effective above ground, in the ocean, and even in the sky, how could it possibly get more powerful? Catria couldn't imagine, but she was sure of at least one thing…

"We'll enter using a Shovel Tunnel, Shovel Railroad, and an underground Shovel Battleship. Yeah, that sounds about right."

Their adventure to the Kingdom of Darkness was going to be something awful.

INTERMISSION
Lithisia's Solo Shovel

BEFORE LEAVING on their journey to the Kingdom of Darkness, Alan and the others decided to rest for the night at the World Tree Castle. They were all rather exhausted from their adventure in Rahzelfo, and even shovels needed rest. Not only had Alan's fired off multiple Wave Motion Shovel Blasts, it had also soaked in the Angel Furnace for quite some time. Shovels were durable and wouldn't break, but it was best to let them rest so they could regain their cutting edge.

Thus, for a while, the team relaxed.

Late in the night, Alan was awake and about; he had gone to bed quite early. "One orb left... Man, I've come a long way..."

There was only a little left to the request Lithisia had first made of him.

Alan thought back on his meeting with the princess. *That's right. When we first met, she...*

"D-don't worry about me! You can't possibly win with just a shovel!"

"How did things turn out like this?"

At the time, Lithisia had been a strong and kind young woman. Now she was a strong and kind shovel woman. The quickness and diversity with which she harnessed the powers of the shovel stunned even Alan, and those powers grew every single day. In only a few weeks, she'd experienced inconceivable growth. Or perhaps "evolution" was the better word.

"I mean, I'm happy and all, but...hrm?"

Just then, he heard a small noise coming from far above, all the way on the roof of the elf castle. Alan had left his shovel up there to let it dry out. Could it be an enemy attack? No, he didn't sense anything of the sort. Nonetheless, he grabbed one of his secondary shovels and fired a Shovel Wire up to the roof. It was an express route.

The moon was full and the stars were as bright as ever. In front of the shovel Alan had stabbed into the stone roof was a single girl in a dress. Lithisia. She was on her hands and knees, carefully blowing onto Alan's shovel, then delicately wiping it down with a silk cloth. She repeated this process over and over again. Finally, she ran her finger along the shovel as if to check her work.

"Hm... It's still kind of dusty...j-just a little more, shovel."

Lithisia restarted the process, sweat glistening on her forehead and dirt staining her knees. Judging by her current state, she'd been polishing this shovel for hours. Lithisia was likely planning on continuing this until morning without a wink of sleep.

Alan watched in silence from the corner of the roof.

"Sir Miner...this is all I can do, but..."

Alan thought to call out to her but stopped himself. Lithisia had taken it upon herself to polish his shovel. It wasn't Alan's place to interfere. She simply and quietly, in the shadows, wanted to give her all to maintaining his shovel.

I should pretend I didn't see anything and get out of here... That was the kindest thing Alan could do as a miner. When it came to anything but romance, he was a man who knew a great deal about the subtleties of the heart. *I should get back to bed.*

He turned his back to Lithisia and prepared to leave. It was then that Lithisia, silk cloth in hand, looked up, cheeks damp with sweat. She seemed on edge, but she hadn't noticed Alan watching her from afar. For some reason, her cheeks were turning slightly red.

"Mm..." After confirming nobody was around, Lithisia brought the silk cloth to her face. With every fiber of her being, she inhaled the aroma of the cloth. "Mmmmmaaaahhh! Sir Miner's shovel scent...his aroma...mmph!"

Her body trembled as her whole being filled with joy. Lithisia kept sniffing as her eyes brimmed with tears. She was completely focused on this experience.

"Mmmmmph, I love it. I love shovels. I love this shovel scent! Mmmmmm!!!"

Scoop, scoop! Scoop, scoop! (The sound of her refilling her Shovel Charge through her nose!)

"What in the hell is that sound?" said Alan.

"?!"

Crap, I didn't mean to interject.

As Lithisia held the cloth up to her nose and once more inhaled, she at last made eye contact with Alan.

Time itself froze, the miner's shovel gleaming in the pale moonlight. Lithisia tightly closed her thighs. Confusion writ itself across her face. *Huh? Sir Miner? Why? Y-you weren't supposed to be here. You weren't here. Why are you here? He saw me, he saw me, he saw my shovel he saw my...*

Thus began the waterworks. Lithisia cried like she had never cried before.

"Noooooo! Scoop, scoop, scoop!" Lithisia waved her hands about, her face colored with mortification. Her entire head was basically a tomato at this point. "I-It's not what it looks like! This isn't a shovel or scoop or a...ah...aaaaaahhh!!!"

"Get a hold of yourself, Lithisia! You're not making any sense!"

"I swear it's not what it looks like, shovel!" Lithisia dashed off at full speed.

It would be bad to let her go in this state, Alan thought, so he grabbed her, placing her arms behind her back. Nonetheless, she continued to resist with all of her might. Where was this tremendous power coming from?!

"Urgh!" Left with no other choice, Alan grabbed the shovel nearby and swung it. "SHOVEL (stop)!"

"!!!"

Lithisia was paralyzed. This was a special skill that capitalized on the fact that both "shovel" and "stop" started with the letter "s."

"Uuuuuuuh..."

Lithisia looked at Alan with tear-filled eyes. Her regret was plainly apparent. She apologized over and over again, wishing she were dead. In the hopes of making her feel safe and perhaps calming her down, Alan took his shovel and caressed the top of her head with it.

"Ah...ahh..."

Lithisia's eyes drooped as Alan continued to rub the head of his shovel across her pate. For some reason, this bizarre princess was more at ease with a shovel than she was a human hand.

"Don't worry, Lithisia. I'm not angry."

"Ah...mm?"

Really, shovel? Even though I'm such a scooping shovel of a princess? So said Lithisia's eyes, but Alan was being honest. Truth be told, he had no clue what she was doing.

Anyhow, by the time Alan brought her back to his room, Lithisia had quieted a bit. She was holding her little red shovel up against her chest, her eyes still watery and her expression uncertain. In Alan's hands was his shining adamantine shovel, perfectly polished.

I suppose I should say this first, Alan thought. "You have my thanks, Lithisia."

"Shovel?!" Lithisia raised her voice in surprise at his expression of gratitude.

"You did one helluva job polishing my shovel. Even I could never get it to shine this bright."

"Um, um...sh-shovel..."

"Not that I'm surprised. You're probably the best shovel polisher on the continent."

"Uuuh, ah..." Lithisia put her hands on her cheeks and squirmed, her gaze cast downward. "Thank you, very shovel..."

She looked flustered, but she also seemed extremely happy.

"And then, um, I'm sorry for peeping on you."

"Nnnngh!!!" Lithisia's body trembled again.

"No, no. Don't worry. I'm not going to pry, I promise."

"Huh? Scoopy? (But why?)"

(Only Alan could have understood her.)

Why? he thought. One reason was that he likely wouldn't understand anyway. Another was that Lithisia herself was so worked up. He didn't really get what was going on, but he knew unearthing a young woman's secrets by force was not a good thing (the noblewoman Lucrezia was a special case in that she enjoyed it).

Lithisia scooped with her shovel. That was all he needed to know.

"Ugh... U-um..." Lithisia appeared to be at ease for a moment, but she didn't leave the room. With her red shovel in hand and an awkward expression, she managed to look Alan directly in the eyes. "I...I have something I want to talk to you about... It's about earlier."

Alan understood this was of great importance to Lithisia. Hell, she hadn't even attached "shovel" to the end of her sentence. Something was different about this. "Are you sure you want to tell me?"

"I-It's embarrassing, but, but, but!" Lithisia squeezed her shovel tightly. "I hate the idea of burying and hiding my secret from you even more, so..."

"Hrm." Alan could do naught but be quiet and listen after hearing her so resolutely say something like that.

"Um, Sir Miner...do you remember our promise?"

"Of course I do."

At the beginning of this journey, Lithisia had sworn an oath. In exchange for Alan helping her search for the orbs, she would do anything he asked. Alan had asked that she gather successors for him, and she agreed to do it.

There was but one orb remaining. The time to fulfill her promise drew near.

"So, um, that's why I was, um, thinking I need to prepare for the big day..."

"The big day?"

"Er, you know... How I'm going to make you a child..."

This was Lithisia's way of saying she was going to "make him a successor." Or at least, that's what Alan had convinced himself she meant. As far as Lithisia was concerned, she meant exactly what she said: birthing his child.

"But I'm not like you," said Lithisia. "I'm just a regular human."

If Catria were present, she would have cut in with an "excuse me?" but fortunately, she wasn't in the room.

"S-so in order for me to, um, successfully scoop and shovel with you..." Lithisia held her red shovel tightly and proclaimed, "I have to become a shovel myself!"

One could argue the conversation had been scooped up and launched into the stratosphere.

Lithisia continued her confession as if the dam of her consciousness had been blown to bits. "That's why I tried to refill my Shovel Charge with your shovel...! A-and then my body got all hot, and I felt like I had to scoop a little with your shovel...ah! I'm so, so sorry!"

Tears poured from her eyes as she apologized profusely.

"I'm so sorry...I'm so sorry I'm such an unbecoming Shovel Princess!" Her face was bright red as she bowed her head again and again while on her knees.

Alan said nothing. Well, it was more like he couldn't find the words. As for why, it was because around the second half of Lithisia's explanation, he'd completely lost track of what she was trying to say. Why did finding him successors mean she'd have to become a shovel?

Even so, he couldn't find it within himself to pry any deeper.

She's serious... He could tell by the tone of her voice and the look in her eyes that she was trying to be honest with him. This young woman in front of him really was trying with all of her might to become a shovel.

"Make Alan a child."

In order to fulfill that singular promise, she was shoveling as best as she could. Every shovel action she took was for that purpose.

I see...

It didn't matter how little Alan understood Lithisia's beliefs, she would persevere and hold true to them. This adherence to her beliefs was one-to-one with Alan's own way of living. A thousand years ago, people had laughed at Alan for implacably digging up jewels. What was the point in doing what he did? Was something wrong with him? But Alan continued. He continued being "weird," and eventually, digging became a part of who he was.

Bowing in front of him was a young woman who knew those same feelings. How could he not want to cheer for her? Support her? Even if he didn't quite understand her motivations, did he need to?

"Lithisia." Alan once again caressed her head with his shovel.

"Ah... Shovel...?"

"Thank you, Lithisia." Alan embraced her delicate body

from behind and squeezed her gently. She was distractingly soft in his arms, but this was important. He then brought the handle of his shovel close to Lithisia's face. She seemed puzzled by his actions, but she was also dazed with joy.

Alan was holding her from behind as if they were lovers. Was she dreaming?

"Ah...um, Sir Miner...?"

"If that's the case, let me do everything I can to help you."

"Huh? Eeeeek?!"

Alan channeled power into his shovel. The gleaming adamantine metal came alight with blue energy, and that energy wrapped around Lithisia's body, lifting her into the air. This Shovel Aura enveloped Lithisia's very being. Alan didn't precisely know what Lithisia meant by refilling her "Shovel Charge," but he imagined this might help.

"How does this feel, Lithisia? Can you feel the shovel?"

"Eeek... Ah..."

Lithisia let herself lean against Alan's chest as she breathed in and out. Her body was being caressed by the shovel. She couldn't have been happier. Lithisia wanted to stay like this forever.

"It's so...shovelly scoop...!"

"That's right. Scoop it is."

"Aaaaaah!"

Alan continued to embrace Lithisia from behind as the Shovel Power ran through her. Her face relaxed, her body grew terribly hot, and she left her heart in Alan's hands.

For the rest of that night, Alan continued to tenderly hold this young woman, this sweet, lovable young woman, in the aura of his shovel.

It was already too late for both of them.

The next morning, when they were about to set off on their next journey, Lithisia came down with a Shovel Fever. She was forced to lay in the carriage pressing a shovel to her forehead to cool down. Nonetheless, she wore an unbelievably happy smile.

"Alan, what did you do to the princess?"

"Hrm, well..."

Alan explained to Catria that the previous night, he saw Lithisia on the roof polishing his shovel to refill her Shovel Charge. She desperately wanted to become a shovel, and after she expressed the earnestness of this desire, he decided to support her with an equally earnest shoveling, and...

"I TAKE IT BACK. I DON'T WANT TO KNOW!" Catria was dripping sweat as she breathed in and out.

Within the carriage, Alice was unconscious. Lucy, meanwhile, had fled to Heaven, at least in her head.

"Are you trying to kill us?!"

"Nooo...the shovels are coming to get us..."

"I'm sorry."

As this stupidity progressed, the party arrived at the border of the Kingdom of Darkness, where they were met with a vast Obsidian Gate that stretched up into the sky. Beyond the wall as tall as a mountain, black smoke floated into the air.

"Excellent. Now then, let's go over the mission once agai..." Alan trailed off. "Huh."

Something was approaching them from the gate. A horse.

"Haaah... Haaah... I can't die here. I refuse to die here!" A bronze-skinned young woman with long black hair rode the animal. She looked a wee bit younger than Lithisia, and as far as Alan could tell, she wore an expensive tiara. The young woman who appeared to be some kind of princess was being pursued by five men in black robes.

"Don't let her go! We'll make bank if we catch her!"

The bronze-skinned princess was apparently a mark.

A princess and her pursuers... This was just like what had happened with Lithisia. That meant Alan had but one course of action available to him.

"DIG!"

KA-CHOOOOOOOOM!

Alan blew away the robed men with his Wave Motion Shovel Blast, causing the bronze-skinned princess to look behind her.

"Huh?" She looked forward, then back again. "What the?!"

She stopped in her tracks, entirely flabbergasted by the change in her situation.

"Catria, we're saving her!"

"I feel like not getting involved qualifies as saving her, but, oh well." Catria sighed and followed after Alan.

This bronze-skinned princess was fleeing from someone just as Lithisia had been, but there was really only one thing Catria was concerned about: would this young woman also be able to escape shovel corruption?

THE INVINCIBLE SHOVEL

Holy Knight Shovel Blade
Equipment: Weapon

RARITY
SSS (Scoopy Shovelly Scoops)

EXPLANATION
A Holy Knight Shovel fashioned into a holy sword for the knight Catria by the miner Alan. Its tip is shaped like an arrowhead in order to mimic the head of a shovel, and it has a handle on its hilt for easy digging. Yelling "DIG" unlocks its true powers, transforming its shape into that of a shovel.

EQUIPMENT EFFECTS
- Attack +145
- Applies the "Holy" attribute to all regular attacks
- Blast Wave Group Attack (each enemy hit at two-thirds full power)

SPECIAL EFFECTS
① Talent Unearthing
Unlocked at SHV Level 20+. After a battle, the user gains two times as much experience. Their chance of learning a new skill is multiplied by three.

② Shovel Blade Awakening
Unlocked at SHV Level 37+. All the power the miner Alan has poured into the sword is unleashed.
On a combat turn equivalent to one's SHV Level, HP, MP, Strength, Stamina, and Dexterity are all multiplied by 4.5, and the skill "Descent of the Mining God" is made available.

At the start of Volume 3, Catria has already unlocked the first ability. By the end of the Volume, she has unlocked the second.

HOLY SHOVEL EMPIRE, OFFICIAL DICTIONARY
(AUTHOR: LITHISIA), 21ST VERSION.

CHAPTER 8

The Kingdom of Darkness' Shovel
(KURONONO'S INTO IT)

PART 37
The Miner Shovels the Bronze-Skinned Princess

I T WAS EARLY in the afternoon, but the sky was black as a host of storm clouds gathered above the Kingdom of Darkness.

After Alan and the others saved the bronze-skinned girl and broke through the Obsidian Gate, they decided to camp in a nearby forest. Alan cut some firewood with his shovel and started a fire using the Shovel Friction. With his Shovel Rifle, Alan took down some wild boar and cooked them. Needless to say, the party were going to sleep in the safety of a Shovel Cave.

"My head hurts..." Catria knew in her heart this adventure was going to suck.

In any event, the party sat around the fire along with the bronze-skinned girl, warming her up.

"Um! Thank you for saving me, Master Mage!" The girl bowed again and again in gratitude. Her name was Kuronono and she was quite young. In fact, it was entirely possible she hadn't yet hit fourteen.

Alan and Catria heard her story out while Lithisia was still resting in the carriage. Meanwhile, Alice and Lucy were in the middle of ascending to the next realm of existence.

"Master Mage, eh?" Alan couldn't help but chuckle. Those were nostalgic words, in a way. When he first showed Lithisia his Wave Motion Shovel Blast, she had mistaken his shovel skills for magic as well. It appeared the shovel's ability to fire Wave Motion Shovel Blasts just wasn't an accepted truth in this world. "Now that I think about it, even you didn't accept that the shovel was a beam weapon when we first met, Catria."

"Of course I didn't."

Normal shovels didn't fire beams. That was supposed to be—er, it *was* common sense.

"Um... Master Mage?"

"My apologies. My name is Alan, Alan the miner. This here is Catria, head of Rostir's Holy Shovel Knights."

"Head of the Holy Knights?!"

"You couldn't be more wrong."

An exclamation point appeared above Kuronono's

head as she looked up at Catria, her gaze filled with respect and longing. "Huh? But aren't you a Holy Knight...?"

"Well, yes. I'm a knight of Rostir, but I'm no Holy *Shovel* Knight."

"A knight of Rostir...! Lady luck is finally on my side!" Tears welled up in Kuronono's hopeful eyes. She corrected her posture and once more bowed deeply to Alan and Catria. "Um! Please save the Kingdom of Darkness! No, um, please save the world, oh heroes from Rostir!"

The party listened as Kuronono explained the dire circumstances of the Kingdom of Darkness. Five years ago, she had been the kingdom's princess, but now she was nothing more than a slave. Demons had led a rebellion against the royal family.

The kingdom was all about mining the mountains and earth, so during Kuronono's childhood they had summoned several tens of thousands of demons to serve this end.

"We used the demons for their labor... But we were wrong."

Even young as she was, Kuronono had been against her father's plan. She knew the ancient magic kingdom had thrived by using demons as an enslaved workforce, but the Kingdom of Darkness' magical technology was nowhere near as advanced as that of the ancients'. Summoning demons was, therefore, far too dangerous, especially in such large numbers. But no matter what the young Kuronono said, her father the king refused to listen.

Then it all fell apart.

The Pleasure Bell that controlled the demons vanished from the Great Cathedral, and with that, everything changed. The king was murdered, and the kingdom's citizens were enslaved just as the demons had been. Now, once humans exhausted themselves in physical labor for the demons, they became demon food. The situation was especially horrifying for women, who were forced to do hard labor until they came of age, after which they became "seedbeds" for the demons.

All the former citizens of the kingdom were doomed to end their lives deep beneath the surface. Even the sky over the mountains was filled with storm clouds created by the demons, so there was no chance anyone would ever see the sun.

"Humans of the Kingdom of Darkness no longer see the light. We have only the fires of Hell to comfort us." Kuronono meant the literal version of Hell. As she trailed off, she tried to hide the pain in her eyes. "Lady Catria, Sir Alan. Please tell your nation what happened here."

"Our nation?"

"Yes, preferably someone of royal blood. Time is of the essence!"

Upon building the Obsidian Gate, the Kingdom of Darkness had been effectively cut off from all communication with the outside world. This had proved to be the key to humanity's ruin. A massive demon army was being cultivated behind that enormous gate. The women who had been turned into "seedbeds" gave birth to more demons for the planned great invasion while the enslaved men continued to forge the demons' weapons.

Soon the demons would be ready to start an all-out war to enslave the rest of humanity.

"Curse it all! How could this be?!" Catria dug her feet into the ground. Was this the reason demons had attacked Rostir as well? "Kuronono, thank you for sharing this with us."

This girl had fled from Hell itself. As a Holy Knight, Catria couldn't look past her plight. Just as she had made her decision...

"I've heard everything, shovel!" Lithisia's voice echoed out from the carriage, immediately dispelling the tense atmosphere.

Kuronono blinked rapidly at the carriage. As she did, Princess Lithisia descended from it, regal of bearing and pure of shovel.

"Your Highness, we're trying to have an adult conversation," said Catria through gritted teeth. "No shoveling or scooping allowed."

"All shovels are adult shovels, Scootria."

Who in the hell was Scootria? The intensity of the princess's shovelness (???) had seemingly grown worse.

"H-huh? Your Highness...?" said Kuronono. "Wait, are you Princess Lithisia?!"

"Scooooop! (That I am!)"

Kuronono couldn't hide her shock.

This is bad, thought Catria. *Should I trick her and tell her we all wear earplugs when addressing the princess?*

No, that would be a step too far, even in the name of the fight against shovelfication.

Lithisia spoke. "Lady Kuronono, you've shoveled well. Please, leave the scooping to us."

"Really?! Ah...thank you, thank you so much!"

"Howshovel!" Lithisia pointed her shovel at Kuronono.

She clearly wanted to say "however." Catria was profoundly sad she could understand that. The princess was literally just substituting any and every word with "shovel," or "scoop," or some variation thereof.

"Now that you've made a formal scooquest of a Shovel Princess, my nation will require adequate payment, shovel!"

"Payment...?"

Alan, who had remained quiet as he stared up at the sky, finally cut in. "Lithisia, that really won't be necessary."

"Sir Miner, you'll have to excuse me, but this is a matter of international business for Rostir. A Shovel Payment is necessary."

"Hm, is that really the case?"

Whatever his doubts, it was true that if this was to be a negotiation of international policy, Alan was obligated to stay out of it.

"That's really the case, scoop. Hee hee..." Lithisia's eyes glowed suspiciously as she drew close to Kuronono's ear and whispered into it.

"Huh?! Eeek!" Kuronono glanced at Alan and in an instant, her bronze skin turned pink.

"This is an official request. Plus, I'm sure you're not against it."

"Um, I...but..."

"Yo, Lithisia," said Alan.

Kuronono was too overwhelmed to process Alan's interruption. She squirmed, turning in on herself with all the shyness due to an inexperienced young woman. But once her line of sight settled on her chest, her expression darkened. She bowed her head apologetically. "I'm sorry, but...I can't do that."

"Don't worry! The shovel doesn't hurt."

"*Lithisia.*"

"That's not it..."

Kuronono, having made her decision, rolled up her upper garments to reveal the stretch of skin from her belly button up to just below her small but shapely chest. What drew the eyes more than anything was the tattooed scarification on her stomach, which was in the shape of a horrific demon.

"Demons use their poisonous body fluids to carve this symbol into the bodies of women who will one day serve them as seedbeds." Traces of blood were yet visible on Kuronono's stomach as she grimaced. It was clear it hurt dreadfully. "A-all who bear this tattoo die if they... are touched by any man who isn't a demon."

"Shoveeeel (rage)."

"Your Highness, quiet."

"But to be honest, Sir Alan...no, any man..." Kuronono lowered her gaze forlornly and smiled. "Any man would think twice before even looking at a woman with a scar like this..."

"Shovel! (That has nothing to do with it!)"

"Your Highness, please show some self-restraint."

"And there's one other problem...ah...nngh..." Slowly but steadily, blood began to seep from Kuronono's scar.

It didn't show any sign of stopping, and indeed grew worse and worse.

"Shovel (worry)?!"

"Your Highness, go home. Are you okay, Kuronono?!"

"No, I...I'm sorry... It looks like I'm out of time..." Kuronono managed to maintain a smile as sweat slid down her temples. "Citizens of the kingdom are...forbidden from leaving..."

The blood flowed ever more intensely. If Kuronono lost any more, it would be fatal. Her scar now glowed a despicable dark red. This was the curse of the demons' tattoo. Yet despite this intense pain, Kuronono continued to gaze at Alan.

"I'm...not long for this world." She couldn't afford to die until she fulfilled her mission. "That's why I beg of you all..."

"Shovel! (Don't speak!)"

"Your Highness, just stop..." groaned Catria. "Wait, no, now's not the time for that! Alan!"

"Roger. I'm good to go."

Alan swept Kuronono up in his arms, and the second he did, a strange sensation overwhelmed her entire body. Nothing hurt anymore. She was warm; the parts of her body being touched by Alan tingled with strange fire. Had her senses completely shorted out?

Was she dying?

"Kuronono, there are two things I have to correct you on."

"Huh…?"

"A woman's true beauty defies the scars of the flesh."

"H-huh?!"

Badump, badump!

"True beauty lies in the depths of one's heart. And in that sense, you're exquisitely beautiful already."

"But, I…I…" Kuronono's heart was racing a mile a minute.

No way. Did this man truly consider her worthy of love, even after she had endured torture, even after this scar had been carved into her body? Alan directed his serious gaze at the grim tattoo on her stomach, as if in direct challenge to her thoughts. She was terribly embarrassed, and her whole body was burning red-hot. But…

"Eeee…"

She was also ecstatically happy. Kuronono would get to leave to the next world whilst being tenderly held by this strong miner. Her heart felt like it was about to melt, even as the strength left her body.

I can't believe it, she whispered in her heart of hearts.

"We're going to shovel, Kuronono."

She swallowed and nodded. She didn't know what that meant, really, she only knew she was going to die.

But if it was something this gentle man was going to do, she didn't mind.

While silently expressing gratitude toward Alan, she closed her eyes.

"DIG!"

In one fell swoop, Alan dug a human-shaped hole and buried Kuronono within it. He left only her face above ground. It kind of resembled when men and women bury themselves on the beach for fun.

"Huh...?" Kuronono stared down at herself. *What the...?*

"I'm removing the poison from you," Alan explained.

Next to him, Catria looked like she had had enough of everything.

"There we go. I've drained the last of the demonic poison. When you drain the poisons from a fish, you bury it in dirt, you know? It's just like that."

"Scooptical! (Wow, what a practical shovel treatment!)"

"Your Highness, you've brought new meaning to the word 'forced.'"

Five seconds later, Alan dug Kuronono up from her hole. Her stomach was still bare, but her demonic tattoo had vanished, her blood no longer flowed from the wound, and her skin was as smooth as it once had been. She even felt healthier; all of her muscle pains were gone.

Kuronono's mouth fell open in astonishment. "Uh... um...*what the*?!"

Her words rang with confusion. She clearly had no idea what had just transpired.

"Now I said I had to correct you on two things. That was the first. For the second, you said that citizens of the Kingdom of Darkness could no longer see light."

"Y-yes, and?!"

"That ends today." Alan pointed his shovel toward the heavens. "DIG!"

A column of light erupted from his shovel, shooting into the sky like a reverse shooting star and smashing through the storm clouds. It was like the sun itself had exploded as rainbow light spread throughout the land.

After that, the true sun revealed itself, illuminating Kuronono's bronze skin. In one blow, Alan obliterated the storm clouds that had drowned the sky.

"From now on, the Kingdom of Darkness will be known as the Kingdom of Light."

Kuronono cast her empty gaze at the sun above. Lithisia watched from afar with a smile on her face. Catria, on the other hand, sighed at the three of them.

See? I knew it. This whole thing is ridiculous.

PART 38
The Miner Makes Kuronono His Bikini Disciple

THE ROYAL CAPITAL of the Kingdom of Darkness, or The One True Steel City, was presently held by demonic forces, and could be found some thousand feet underground. Alan and the party made their way toward it in the SS *Scoop*, their supersized underground battleship. At full power, its Wave Motion Shovel Engine could drill all the way to Hell in a single second.

This vessel was Alan's secret weapon, a moving home base he had developed for the express purpose of adventuring through Hell. It had a ten-bedroom layout with multiple bathrooms and half-baths. The cockpit even had a meeting room built adjacent to it. All in all, it was the perfect living space.

"Seriously...?" On hearing all this, Catria groaned, her head starting to hurt.

Alan, meanwhile, dug into parallel space at high speed. The Wave Motion Shovel Engine's total output was directly proportional to Alan's own shovel output.

Catria didn't even know where to start. "What's with this joke of a ship...? I mean, is it even a ship?"

As far as Catria's common sense was concerned, ships were meant to sail upon water. This idiot thing was digging through the earth.

"Horse carriages can fly through the air, but they can't dig beneath the surface, so we had to use this," said Alan.

"Horse carriages usually can't fly through the air!"

But no matter how much Catria pushed back, the metal cockpit before her wasn't going to be defeated with words. Trying to speak to this man with normal language was an exercise in futility.

"Fine, whatever... So, are you planning on conquering the kingdom with this thing?"

Catria had no doubt the absurd ship in question could probably take down tens of thousands of demons in a matter of seconds.

But Alan shook his head. "According to Kuronono, a resistance organization is fighting against the demon occupation. We're going to work with them."

It was a small but determined organization, one

Kuronono had been a part of. Their power had enabled her to escape and get her message out.

"Do we really have to work with them?"

"Of course. People have to be allowed to liberate themselves with their own power where possible. Catria, just think back on your fight with the Mage King."

Catria frowned. She had indeed gained a great deal of confidence through defeating the Mage King without Alan's help. Furthermore, the fact of the matter was that Catria was much stronger now than she had been when she first met Alan, especially when it came to mental fortitude. If she had relied on Alan all this time, she wouldn't have gained any of those abilities.

"In order for the Kingdom of Darkness to truly rise again, they can't rely on me to save them," said Alan.

Similarly, in her efforts to revitalize elven civilization, Fio worked long and hard all on her own. Alan was just lending her a hand now and then.

"I guess that makes sense..."

Ninety percent of this guy's crap was full of shovels, but 10 percent of it made sense. Although, in Princess Lithisia's case, 300 percent of anything she said was Shovel Crap. She was already three times more shovel-tastic than should ever be allowed.

"By the way, Alan. Where's the girl of the hour?" Catria asked.

"I sort of ruined her clothes, so I asked Lithisia get her a new outfit."

Catria felt a chill in her bones. She shook her head rapidly to get rid of the sensation.

No, she wouldn't dare. Sure, the princess is kind of berserking these days, but even she wears a pure, classy dress! She's never once ordered me to change out of my knight armor into some kind of Shovelwear.

It would be fine. The princess generally didn't step past a certain line. She wouldn't make a teenager wear anything weird.

Catria repeated this to herself over and over again, but eventually she turned to find a bronze-skinned young girl (tinted a demure red) wearing a pink micro bikini. Kuronono's legs were stuck together straight as a board and she was rocking back and forth uncomfortably.

"Sorry to keep you waiting! I present to you, a very scoopy little Kuronono!" Lithisia explained from off to the side with a big smile.

"WHAT ARE YOU MAKING HER WEAR, YOUR HIGHNESS?!"

"Eeeee..." Kuronono squirmed. Her bikini didn't

cover nearly as much as her original outfit had, and rather obviously it was far more troubling.

Alan was so stunned by the sight that the Shovel Engine ground to a halt.

"Fear not, Catria!" declared Lithisia. "This is just diplomacy between the royalty of two nations!"

"Your Highness, I formally request that you apologize to every diplomat in the world."

"And anyway, Kuronono requested shothes (Shovel Clothes) herself."

The bronze-skinned princess sidled over to Alan's side and looked up at him as she blushed. "Am I...scoop enough?"

Alan was seized by an ungodly headache. "How did it come to this?"

Kuronono seemed puzzled. "Didn't you know Rostir's condition for assistance was that I 'offer my scoopy body to Sir Alan'?"

"Why...?"

"Sir Miner, allow me to explain, shovel!"

And so Lithisia did. Since times long past, Rostir and the Kingdom of Darkness had no formal communication or interaction with one another. Lithisia and Kuronono's meeting was the beginning of a new relationship. In order to affirm their bond as new sister nations, Lithisia wanted Kuronono to be shoveled by Alan, just like she would be.

"And so I had her promise to 'shovel' with you for the first time."

"Y-yes, exactly!"

Lithisia pushed Kuronono forward as she explained, the younger girl's cheeks bright red.

Ohhhhh, Alan thought to himself.

The so-called promise to "shovel" he had made with Lithisia (as far as he was concerned, anyway) was that she would "create a successor" for him, i.e., she was going to gather candidates to be his apprentice. But Lithisia was more than capable enough of doing that on her own. He also couldn't figure out why a search for an apprentice involved putting Kuronono in a bikini.

"Sir Miner, Kuronono is fantastically shoveltractive!"

"Putting aside your failure to use human words, I already said she was beautiful."

Wait a second.

"Don't tell me you mean to have me take her back to the mountain with me?"

Lithisia nodded firmly.

Did the princess mean this very girl was to be Alan's successor? But Kuronono was still so young, and royalty of a foreign nation at that!

No, perhaps that was exactly why Lithisia had chosen her. Kidnapping the royalty of an enemy nation and taking them home as political hostages was certainly one form of diplomatic strategy. And after all, Alan's mountain and the space beneath it were technically part of Rostir's territory. If Alan had the princess of a foreign kingdom work with him, it would establish a certain hierarchy between the two countries.

"But then what's the point of this absurd bikini?"

Kuronono inched forward and slowly removed the hands covering her exposed skin as she strengthened her resolve. "U-um... I thought...if I showed you my body... I...could have you decide whether or not I can 'shovel'..."

"Aha."

In other words, Kuronono wanted Alan to assess the movement of her muscles. It was indeed true that mining involved hard labor, so having good Shovel Form was critical. If Alan was going to raise a disciple, he would have to carefully monitor their body, and in that sense, a micro bikini was ideal training gear since it rendered Kuronono's musculature wholly visible.

I get it now. Nothing about this is creepy, Alan decided.

Nothing about this was creepy *at all*.

"I'm unforgiving (as an instructor)," he told Kuronono. "Are you okay with that?"

Kuronono's frail body shivered but her resolve remained unshaken.

"If you need my body...my damaged body..." Kuronono touched one of the scars she yet bore from torture. She clenched her fists. "I'd be happy to offer myself to your shovel, Sir Alan."

Her expression was tense, but one could make out the faint light of curiosity in her eyes.

"I'm prepared. I know I'm ignorant of much, and inexperienced, but I leave myself in your capable hands!"

"All right. Then let me get you a shovel." With that, Alan whipped one of his spare shovels and presented it to Kuronono.

"Huh...?"

"What is it? If you're going to follow me, you're going to need one."

Kuronono stared at the object in silence for a long moment before nodding. "I-I'm not sure I understand, but, um, I'm going to use this shovel, right?"

"Correct. Make sure you get your body used to it."

"Get used to...this? It's so...big, but, um, I'll do my best..."

Something is deeply wrong here. Catria sensed some sort of awful shovel misunderstanding was currently underway, but she dedicatedly kept her mouth shut and stuck in her earplugs. This miner and princess would never listen to her words of basic human logic.

"Okay, Kuronono. It's about time you lead us to the resistance base."

"Yes, of course! Gosh, I hope everyone's okay..."

Alan saw the worry on her face and patted her head.

"It's going to be okay, Kuronono. When it comes to matters of the underground..." The miner gripped his shovel. "The shovel is invincible."

"Shing! (Shovmazing! (Sir Miner's shovel is so amazing that it's invincible!))" Lithisia's translation was only getting worse.

"And first of all, is there any place where your dumb shovel isn't invincible?" Catria moaned.

But Catria's words were swallowed by the sounds of the Shovel Drill.

And so the party headed deep below the surface, to the hellish nation ruled by demons...

PART 39
The Princess Holds a Shovelive

DEEP WITHIN A PRISON surrounded by boiling magma was a red-haired girl in chains with no clothes to speak of.

"Kuro..."

She was the head of the resistance, Odessa. Her body was caked in blood from countless whippings and every one of her nails was horrifically cracked. This was the end result of torture. In the demons' search for Kuronono, they had subjected Odessa to the most brutal of interrogations.

A clump of blood rose in her throat. Had Kuronono managed to see the light of day? She could think of nothing else.

The only thing left in this country was despair. If nothing else, Odessa wanted the tiny princess to see the light of the outside world. That had been her sole desire as she helped the girl flee. The whole thing about "delivering a message to the outside world" had been nothing more than a ruse to convince Kuronono to leave her comrades.

The kingdoms of man stood no chance against these terrifying demons. Even a thousand soldiers would be instantly massacred by a single higher demon, and the sad fact was that over three hundred thousand of those very creatures now occupied the Kingdom of Darkness. Humanity was finished.

"Argh…"

Odessa's heart was already broken, but she somehow clung to consciousness by calling out Kuronono's name.

"Nono…"

"It's time. Get up."

A demon dragged Odessa upright. She was to be subjected to yet another round of endless agony. Sharp claw tips pierced her head, flooding her with intense heat. The inside of her brain was being toyed with. Her tears wouldn't stop—tears not of pain, but of powerlessness.

The demon's voice and her own internal voice overlapped.

The revolution failed. Why? Because you weren't strong enough.

Odessa knew she was far from strong enough. She wanted more strength. Needed it, needed power...power a human could never hope to possess.

"The thirst is strong in this one. She will make for a good seedbed."

With all the brainwashing, Odessa couldn't tell the demon was smiling. The desire for power had been implanted within her so she could become the best possible seedbed.

Her consciousness was fading, along with her life as a thinking human. At the end of it all, she called out a single name. "Kuronono..."

Gods above, I beg of you. At least allow her to see the light.

In that moment, for some reason Odessa's vision blurred. A vision of Kuronono appeared before her.

I must be dreaming... She's smiling... She must've made it, then... I'm so glad... I can see her so clearly... She's wearing a pink micro bikini... She looks so embarrassed, the way she's holding that shovel between her thighs... Wait a second.

"WHY IS SHE IN A BIKINI, AND WHAT'S WITH THE SHOVEL?!"

The second Odessa snapped to her senses and cried out, she could hear Kuronono's voice accompanied by an explosion of some kind. The demon standing before Odessa had been blown to fine particulate matter, and from behind it appeared the princess alongside a man Odessa did not recognize. The princess was wearing an outrageously inappropriate bikini, and she looked unspeakably shy about it.

As soon as Kuronono saw Odessa, she trotted over. "Odessa! Odessa! Hang in there!"

"Argh... Is it really you, Kuronono?! Why are you dressed like that?!"

"Huh!?! U-um, a lot has happened since I left!"

That really didn't explain anything. Odessa wanted to say as much, but she realized now wasn't the time. "Kuronono, why did you come back?! You must flee this place at once!"

The princess and the man accompanying her had managed to take out one of the torturers by a stroke of luck. The torturers were nothing compared to the true demon knights, however.

"Enemy attack! Enemy attack! Teleportation Alert!"

The eerie clanging of an enormous bell echoed throughout the underground. The open plaza in front of the cells soon flooded with a horde of demons over a hundred strong. They howled into the dark air as they charged Odessa's cell.

This is bad! They've already been found!

"Ah! Sir Alan, the enemy's coming!" Kuronono cried.

"Perfect. Just do exactly as I said."

"R-right!" Clad in her bikini, Kuronono raised her small shovel above her head.

"You bastard! What are you making her do?!" snarled Odessa.

"Shovel," said the man.

A beam of light blue energy fired from Kuronono's shovel, completely obliterating three demons who had dared approach Odessa's cell.

"I-I did it, Sir Alan!" Kuronono exclaimed as she clutched her shovel and struck a cute pose. *Th-this is awkward, but it's my responsibility now!*

As for why Alan had taught Kuronono Shovel Combat? Well, on the way to the prison, Kuronono spoke to Lithisia about this very matter. She took Lithisia's sagely words to heart; the truth was clear to her now.

Sir Alan likes girls in bikinis who fight with shovels!

In a short time, her shovel corruption had grown to an absurd level.

"Huh…?" Odessa's eyes rolled back in her head in bewilderment.

"Heh, all I did was give you a nudge, and you've already developed these skills?" said Alan. "Your potential is second only to Catria's, Kuronono."

"R-really?!"

"Yes, even your shovel form was youthful and energetic. Oh, and your quads in particular have room for further growth."

"Ah, um, er, eeek." Kuronono fidgeted.

Odessa, on the other hand, was still unable to move in addition to being deeply appalled. However, she also saw the incoming legion of demons and yelled at Alan. "Get out of here! Just because you managed to defeat a few demons..."

"Now then, Kuronono. Watch and learn." In the next moment, Alan's Shovel Power exploded into the air. "DIG!"

KA-CHOOOOOOOOOM!

Shotgun Wave Motion Shovel Blast. A dozen currents of light blue energy swallowed the demons whole, disintegrating the lot of them.

Kuronono couldn't help but raise her voice, impressed by the sight before her. "Oh my gosh! Sir Alan's shovel is amazing!"

"All right, let me unlock your chains," Alan said to Odessa as he posed with his shovel. (Note: It was a mind-bogglingly cool pose.)

The chains on Odessa's wrists and ankles fell to the floor with a clank, and her cell door popped open. All locks had keyholes, and if the keyhole was destroyed, so too was the lock. That was why the almighty shovel, ruler over all holes, could destroy them at will. It was simple logic.

Alan reached his hand out to Odessa, who was still more or less petrified. "You're the head of the resistance, Odessa? I'm here to save you."

The mysterious man with a shovel and the bikini-clad shovel girl Kuronono who followed his orders... Odessa stared at the two of them and thought to herself, *How did all of this happen?*

Upon saving Odessa, Alan and Kuronono fled with her to a grand dining hall within the underground.

At present, Catria and Lithisia were acting as a separate squad and using the underground battleship SS *Scoop* to free another mountain in the kingdom. Catria's shovel power was already impressive, and when she teamed up with Lithisia, the two of them could easily take down some two hundred demons all on their own, the only problem of course being that Catria's eyes would look dead the whole time. Oh well!

Here, meanwhile, Odessa and Kuronono were reunited in the dimly lit room, which pulsed with the unholy glow of a nearby magma river. Odessa, the red-haired girl, huddled in a chair. Though she had been naked in her cell, she was now attempting to cover up with a spare cape she had found.

"Odessa! I'm so glad you're okay! I...I...!" Kuronono hugged her with tears in her eyes.

"W-wait just a second, Kuronono. I'm not sure I understand what's going on."

In particular, Odessa couldn't wrap her head around the dubiously tiny pink micro bikini the princess was wearing.

Kuronono waved away Odessa's fears and explained everything in a way she thought above reproof, but her tale of Wave Motion Shovel Blasts, underground Shovel Ships, and "shoveling" with miners only left Odessa with her head in her hands.

That didn't answer anything! Now I just have more questions!

Quite frankly, Kuronono's words were harder to deal with than the demons' brainwashing.

"Kuronono, why don't you stop there for now," said Alan. "We have to let Odessa rest."

"Yeah... I feel more exhausted than I did after getting tortured..." Odessa slumped out of her chair to curl up on her side right on the unforgiving stone floor. Just then, she realized her sizable breasts were completely visible. *Ah, that's right. They took my clothes.*

This strange miner was still in the room, but Odessa didn't have the energy to cover up. Kuronono hurriedly stood and threw Odessa's cape over her.

"I-I'm sorry, Odessa. I forgot you still have no clothes. Ah! That's right! I have an extra set." Kuronono rummaged through the paper bag beside her. The first thing she pulled out was a white string of some kind. It was attached to a thin piece of fabric with a ribbon.

In other words, it was another micro bikini.

"…"

Kuronono bowed her head apologetically. "It's small, but it should stretch! I-I know it's a little much, but it's better than being naked!"

I'd rather be naked, Odessa said in her mind before at last falling unconscious.

As Odessa slept, she achieved an inner tranquility that allowed her to listen to Alan's explanation once she woke. She remained silent for a full thirty minutes during his tale.

"I'm just going to split the difference here and pretend I understand for the most part," Odessa said at last.

"I'm glad you're quick on the uptake," Alan said.

"I'm not."

This was what Odessa had surmised: this bikini business was all Alan's weird taste, and the shovel was some kind of bizarre magic. She had completely misunderstood everything, but at this point, nobody had the energy (or the inkling) to correct her.

More importantly, every second they sat around talking, humans were being murdered by the demons. They had to kickstart this revolution as soon as possible.

It was for that very reason that Odessa, as the resistance leader, was needed. Her resolve was particularly crucial.

But Odessa despondently shook her head. Her heart had been temporarily confused by the shovel, but at the end of the day, her own powerlessness was carved into her soul. "There's no point... We have no weapons, and our morale is at rock-bottom... We can't defeat the demons. We never could."

Odessa had spent years trying to come up with strategies and tactics to lead her people to freedom, but it was impossible. Humans were inferior creatures. This was true in terms of strength, weapons, and knowledge. But the biggest problem of all was that...

"The resistance...doesn't exist anymore."

She meant this literally. Odessa and Kuronono were the only remaining survivors of "Humanity's Fangs," the anti-demon resistance force. Everyone else had been captured by the demons. Everything went up in (literal) flames three days ago, when the entire resistance was gathered at their secret base to look into the development of anti-demon weapons. In the middle of their meeting, a fireball was launched directly into the hideout, incinerating most of their organization.

Those who survived met an even more horrible fate. Ever since the demons had gained control of the Kingdom of Darkness, a river of magma had come to flow just beneath it. All through the kingdom, crevasses opened straight to it. The remaining members of the resistance had been tossed into one of these crevasses while they were still alive.

The only ones left were Odessa and Kuronono.

"Ngh...!"

"Kuronono, I'm sorry you had to hear it like this, but... I'm sorry. There's no hope left." Odessa smiled bleakly.

It had taken her three years to build the resistance. With them, Odessa had friends and comrades. She had Kuronono. They were why she had been able to fight for so long. But as she saw each and every person she cared about thrown into the magma, her fighting spirit burned away to nothingness.

I'm...no, all humanity is helpless. That's all we are.

Kuronono embraced Odessa. "I'm so, so sorry. I didn't know. It must've been so hard for you..."

The princess felt her own tears dripping onto her skin. Odessa also began to cry. Kuronono's tears...were warm.

That's why I tried my best to save her. Even her tears are like sunshine. I wanted to make a world where everyone could smile... Odessa thought.

But this world had little room for the brightness of fantasies and fairy tales. Odessa let out a wail of despair.

"They dumped your friends into the magma, eh?" said Alan. "Got it. One sec, lemme scoop them out."

"Excuse...me?"

With a clank, Alan hoisted up his shovel and jogged over to a nearby crevasse running through the dining hall. He thrust his shovel straight into the molten red current of the magma coursing within.

Kersplash!

Almost as if he were pulling a fish from the water, a woman appeared.

"DIG!"

As soon as Alan shouted, the magma around her instantly dispersed.

The woman was no stranger to Odessa. She was in fact Ezel, her very best friend and one of the most important members of the resistance. What's more, she was breathing!

"Huh...?"

What had just happened?

"It's a good thing we're underground. Up top, my shovel can't do anything about the dead."

Alan had used more or less the same technique on the village elder in the desert nation. Alan was incapable of manipulating life and death, but he was capable of uncovering the "past" of the underground. The Kingdom of Darkness existed underground; therefore, its entire history was scoopable. Alan explained this as he continued to scoop up magma.

Soon, all the key members of the resistance were present and accounted for in their original forms.

Odessa, on the other hand, could barely move an inch.

Meanwhile, Ezel sat up, rubbing her bleary eyes. "Where...am I?"

"I can't believe it...Ezel?!"

She's alive! She's okay! I don't understand what's going on, but who cares! She's alive! Odessa was so moved she was on the verge of embracing her best friend.

Before she could do so, Ezel opened her mouth to speak. "Er, Odessa...? Wh-whoa! What are you wearing?!"

"Huh? Ah...EEEK!!!"

Not only was the cloth of Odessa's white bikini dreadfully thin, it was digging into her breasts and hips. In a panic, Odessa tried to cover herself up as Alan's scooping continued in the background. Rather, it came to a stop. He had by now saved everyone from the magma.

"What the heck...?!"

Odessa's eyes were spinning. All of a sudden, the dead had come back to life with no visible harm to suggest they hadn't always been the way they now were. No humans on the planet wouldn't have been shell-shocked.

"All done. Odessa, you said you needed weapons, too, right?"

"Sir Alan, you're incredible! Amazing!" said Kuronono.

"W-wait just a minute! Hold on! I'm...I'm extremely confused!"

But Alan did not wait, and he did not hold on. "Shovels of the deep ground, assemble!"

Upon Alan's order, the shovels lying about the dining hall—had they always been there?—came together as if magnetized. Simultaneously, words were being carved into the handles of the shovels at hyper-speed, the same two words, over and over: "Demon Shoveler."

At last, the silver shovels shone beautifully in the light. Alan thrust one of those shovels into the wall as he yelled out, "DIG!"

At his command, the shovel burrowed through the wall, revealing a lurking demon spy. The second the tip of the shovel made contact with its target, the demon evaporated in a flash of white.

"They're mass-produced models, but they should work well enough. Odessa, how does a hundred thousand of these things sound? Would that be enough?"

"Wait. Seriously, please, just wait a—WHOOOAAA?!"

Odessa had to believe she was dreaming. Shovels were resurrecting people left and right, and now they were killing demons. How could something this convenient just pop up out of nowhere?

But the reality of the situation was that this man, Alan, was creating new weapon after new weapon before her very eyes. The dining hall was filling up with shovels.

"Okay, so when you want to use a shovel, you have to focus and think, 'I'm gonna dig!' as powerfully as you can..." Kuronono explained as she doled out Demon Shovelers to the resurrected resistance.

"This is...crazy," mumbled Odessa.

Madness. This was impossible. How could this be happening?

"How could something straight out of a fairy tale possibly occur...?"

Alerted by the clamor of people and shovels, demons charged into the room, only to be eradicated by Alan after he shouted "DIG!" and fired off a beam of light.

The resistance members gazed as one upon this man and all of a sudden began to chant.

"ALAN! ALAN! ALAN!"

It was as if they were offering prayer to a deity who had just descended to the underground.

"Ah..." Odessa's mouth worked silently.

Alan decimated demons in an instant. Maybe he really was a deity? Perhaps this shovel man was the god who would repel the despair settling upon the Kingdom of Darkness.

No, this is impossible. But, but! I want to believe!

"All right," said Alan. "Last but not least, you needed the morale to stand against the demons, right?"

"Sir Alan! In that case, you can leave it to me! Lady Lithisia taught me everything I need to know!" declared Kuronono.

"She did...?" asked Alan. *I have a bad feeling about this.*

But Kuronono's eyes were twinkling, and as her teacher, he wasn't about to tear her down when she was motivated.

"All right, yeah. Give it a shot. I'll help however you need me to."

"Thank you!"

And so within moments a shage was erected in the dining hall. That's right, a shage, a stage made using shovels. It took only a handful of seconds to build thanks to Alan's Shovel Construction skills. It was about ten feet tall with sheekers (a variant of speakers; releases sound through the dirt) and a large scooplight up above.

Alan dug up and collected spectators from all across the underground. He was able to gather three thousand people with no great deal of trouble.

"Thank you all so much for gathering here today!"

In the center of the shage was Kuronono, still clad in her pink micro bikini, her cheeks bright red from exhilaration and nervousness. Despite her appearance, she did her best to smile as she brought her shovel close to her mouth. "Let's get this underground Shovelive started!"

The crowd Alan gathered raised their voices.

"What is that?"

"A concert?!"

"Is Kuronono gonna sing?"

"Holy bajeebus, she's dressed so weird!"

"Weird but cute!"

"I LOVE YOU, KURONONO!"

The passion in the crowd was infectious.

"KURONONO! SHONONO! SHOVEL! SHOVEL!"

Behind the princess was a man with a shovtar and a man with shovdrums. Kuronono hugged her shovel to herself, knees shaking as she struggled to find the courage to carry out Lithisia's plan.

Lithisia's idea was to hold a "Shovelive." Yes, a "a Shovel Live Performance." Kuronono would raise the troops' morale by dancing and singing in a micro bikini. However, she was soon overwhelmed by the intensity of the entire scenario and was now just kind of wriggling around with the shovel. All the movement caused the strings of her bikini to loosen, which made her panic and cover up.

The crowd cheered even more. The concert was a resounding success.

"U-um, please don't shake the shage too much, or it'll come off!"

"WE LOVE YOU! KURONONO IS LOVE. LOOOOVE!"

"Eeeeek!"

The shage shook even more violently as the crowd stomped their feet with glee.

Meanwhile, Alan and Odessa watched this all take place from backstage.

"I have questions about the method, but...group morale has most certainly gone up, Odessa."

The aforementioned Odessa was on the verge of blacking out. She had a hard time reconciling that she was actually experiencing any of this. The last ten minutes had caused her brain to go into overload; it felt like the insides of her skull had been run through a blender.

Amidst the white void that was her mind, she remembered her own words from not too long ago.

"How could something straight out of a fairy tale possibly occur...?"

Kuronono was wearing a bikini, clinging to a shovel, and dancing before Odessa's very eyes. Each time her bikini threatened to come loose, the crowd erupted into cheers.

As Odessa listened to those excited voices, she realized something important. What was happening in front of her was all too real. And it was no fairy tale.

"E-everyone! Do you really love me that much?!"

"LOVE! LOVE! LOVE! LOVE!"

Indeed, it was no fairy tale. In fact, it was something much darker. Much worse.

PART 40
The Miner Makes a Dungeon With His Shovel

I T ONLY TOOK HALF A DAY for Kuronono's Kingdom of Darkness Shovel Squad to take back the capital from the demons. The princess herself led the charge (a champion in her micro bikini, even if she was embarrassed as all get out). Behind her trailed excited men wielding Demon Shovelers that fired powerful beams of light; it took no time at all to demolish the forces of Hell.

Back at the grand dining hall, those very same men were celebrating their victory.

"Thank you so much, everyone! You all looked so valiant out there with your shovels!" Kuronono stood on shage and raised her shovel, a heroic smile on her face as the micro bikini continued to dig into her skin.

The passion in the dining hall was overwhelming.

"LOVE! LOVE! KURONONO LOVE!"

The Kingdom of Darkness was a country built beneath the surface of the earth itself. In total, its territory included twelve mountains. The One True Steel City where Odessa and the others had been held was a six-thousand-foot tall mountain not unlike an ant hill; it sprawled with rooms and passageways.

And yet it took them a mere half day to free it from the tyrannical rule of the demons.

"Oh happy, happy day! All hail Lady Kuronono! All hail Lady Odessa!"

"H-hey, wait a minute!"

The crowd tossed Odessa into the air, but her mind was still in shambles. It seemed Alan had only just brought out his shovel, yet the revolution had begun and now it was ended.

What...what happened?! I don't understand a single thing that happened today!

"Lady Odessa! Oh, thank you so much! I never thought this day would come...!"

"Aaaahhh!! I love you! I've always loved you, Adelle. Let's get married!"

"Of course, Abel!"

Two of Odessa's closest friends embraced each other in tears. The woman had been torn away from her lover, and the accursed seedbed symbol had been carved into her stomach. That symbol was removed via shovel, allowing her to reunite with her beloved. The couple was overjoyed, of course. They hugged as they shared a passionate kiss.

They truly looked happy.

"Ah...urgh..." Odessa held her head in her hands. *What the heck is a shovel? This is weird. This is completely weird. But everyone's smiling...*

Odessa's dream of five years was unfolding before her very eyes. How could she dismiss the immense joy she was witnessing?

"Ngh..."

The shovel was amazing. It would save humanity.

Maybe I should just learn to accept this... No, I have to.

As Odessa did combat with her reservations, she turned to speak to Alan, who stood next to her. "Alan, as the leader of the r-resistance, I offer you my deepest gratitude..."

It was at least true that she was grateful to him. Without this man's power, the revolution would have failed. Regardless of how absurd his power was, it was still power.

"Odessa, it's way too early to be offering me thanks. Save it for after we've freed the remaining eleven mountains."

"O-of course, you're right. In that case, we should start planning..."

"But before we go on the attack, let's strengthen our defenses in the capital. The stream of demons coming from Hell is pretty much endless."

"Strengthen our defenses? How so?"

"We'll create a barrier to block their invasion into the underground. In other words, we're going to make a dungeon."

Odessa took a moment to think before shaking her head. "We tried that already; it didn't work…"

The Kingdom of Darkness was originally a country of miners. Building a maze to keep invaders out was a practice with which they were both familiar and adept. In fact, they had created a twenty-eight-floor dungeon surrounding the capital city: the "Unending Maze." Though filled with traps, it hadn't been enough to stop the demon invasion. The evil bastards broke through the maze and made quick work of the traps, overwhelming what they couldn't solve with sheer force of numbers.

Odessa tried to explain as much to Alan, but his confidence didn't dim in the slightest.

"Odessa, that only happened because you folks didn't know how to properly build a dungeon."

"What do you mean?"

"As a citizen of the underground, it's in your best interest to memorize this. A true dungeon…" Alan pierced the dirt wall with his shovel and a roar filled the air as the wall morphed into a shining green metal. Alan had buried the molecular structure of the dirt wall and turned it into adamantine using atomic arrangement. Shovel atomic conversion. This was an absolutely necessary technique when it came to building advanced dungeons. "...Can keep out anyone, even the gods themselves."

The wall is made of adamantine now...?

"Urgh!"

Odessa did her best to suppress the urge to dive into a river of magma. Only the profound willpower she'd built up through countless torture sessions allowed her to retain her sanity.

You're okay. Calm down, me. Your mind's been corrupted by shovels, but your body hasn't. Get a hold of yourself and take a good long look at yourself in the mirror. See? You're still you. You're still...human...? Huh?

"A bikini...?"

Indeed, she was still human. In fact, she was basically a human in her birthday suit, only worse. Odessa was still wearing a white micro bikini. The impact of the shovel revolution had caused her to completely forget the shameful state of her attire.

I might already be a lost cause.

Alan examined a 3D map of the twenty-eight-floor Unending Maze surrounding the capital that he was projecting from the metal tip of his shovel.

"I-It doesn't matter how sturdy the walls are, it won't be enough," said Odessa.

Adamantine walls could largely stand against the strength of individual demons, but they weren't an absolute defense. If the demons came at adamantine with all of their power, it inevitably failed.

"Hrm. Odessa, there are three basic qualities a dungeon must have."

"And they are?"

"The first is... All right, perfect timing. Some demons just got through."

As Alan pointed at the map, ten little red lights began to flash. The lights broke through the first floor of the dungeon with a quickness, infiltrating the second floor in mere minutes.

"It took only three minutes to get past the first floor. Odessa, do you know what needs to happen now?"

"I don't."

"We need to use a shovel."

"I still don't."

Alan channeled power into his shovel. The tool shone and Alan dug his way into the dungeon.

Shoop, shoop, shoop!

In about five seconds, Alan had returned and there was now a twenty-ninth floor on top of the twenty-eighth floor on the map.

There was another...floor?

Meanwhile, the demons were still wandering the halls of the second floor.

"We have to outpace the intruders by building more floors," said Alan.

"Wait."

"There's no time for waiting. The first basic quality of a dungeon is that it is 'infinite.'"

"No, seriously. Wait."

"Are you worried about space issues? Don't worry. By tapping something with the head of my shovel, I can 'expand' space-time in the ground. We can build as large a dungeon as we want."

Odessa felt like airholes were being punched into her brain. But she did her best to persist. "Um, Alan, only you're capable of doing that. Humans can't. Get me?"

"Don't worry about that, either. Our Shovel Squad can handle this."

The miner called over Kuronono and her twenty-person Shovel Squad, and explained to them the first basic quality of a dungeon was its "infinitude." The members of the squad of course complained that this was impossible and that Alan was weird in the head.

Thank goodness, they still have common sense.

But just as Odessa felt relief, Kuronono made her move.

"U-um, everyone!" Kuronono stood pigeon-toed, her knees closed together. She bent backward, her small chest thrust out, and held her shovel to hide her mouth, overcome with shyness. "Um, I really, really love when you all try to do the impossible... Y'know?"

"LOVE! LOVE! LOVE!"

Flaming shovels lit up in the squad's eyes and with that, they instantly dug to the dungeon. They weren't as fast as Alan, but they were a sight to behold. A new, thirtieth floor of the dungeon began to appear on the map and in about two minutes, it was finished.

"Thank you all so much! Make sure you practice really hard so you can do it even scoopily faster!"

"LOVE! KURONONO IS LOVE! MUST PRACTICE SCOOPS!"

Odessa gripped her head in her hands, but Alan continued.

"The second basic quality of a dungeon is its 'economic efficiency.'"

Alan flourished his shovel to create tens of Shovel Soldiers. However, these were different from his usual oeuvre. They each held an abacus, and also had tens of shovels strapped to their backs with price tags attached.

"Welcome! What're you buyin'?" one of them said.

These Shovel Soldiers would serve as store clerks.

"Dungeon excavation is hard work, which means people need to be paid. We're going to extract that money from the invading demons."

"Wait just a second."

"There's no time for waiting! Time is money!" said Alan.

"No, seriously. Wait just a second."

But Alan did not wait. He snapped his fingers and the Shovel Soldiers spread throughout the dungeon. Some set up shop by the entrance, selling the demons shovels in exchange for jewels, souls, or even demon currency known as "macca." All this money would go to paying the miners as well as for food. With this setup, the dungeon would be able to function infinitely.

"Economic efficiency is key to getting an infinite dungeon up and running...hm? What's the matter, Odessa?"

A headache. Her head throbbed as if someone had bashed it with a shovel as hard as they could.

"Anyway, onward. The last basic quality of a dungeon. Odessa, do you know what it is?"

"I know nothing."

"Precisely."

"Huh?"

"The most important thing about a dungeon is that the invader keeps getting turned around so often that they have no clue what's going on."

Alan focused energy into his shovel and began to dig. A great rumbling erupted from the earth, as if the capital itself were shaking. This was Alan "randomizing" the dungeon. By doing so, he was rearranging the traps, shops, and general layout of the maze.

Crustal movement via earthquake. By using a shovel, one could initiate this artificially. The shovel was king of the underground, capable of complete manipulative supremacy.

"A dungeon with the same layout won't last forever. That's why you randomize.'"

A dungeon had to be everchanging, otherwise it would fall to anyone who could map it. Randomization was the most important quality a dungeon could have.

"Randomizing a dungeon is a fairly high-level technique, but with Kuronono at the head of operations... What's wrong, Odessa?"

Odessa's brain was moving a mile a minute, on the

verge of dishing out a million descriptions of how insane this all was.

This is nothing like the dungeons I'm familiar with.

She wanted to say as much, but she couldn't grasp the degree of insanity with words. Her head had been dug out entirely.

"Phew..."

It really is too late for me. I'm sorry, Kuronono, Odessa said in her heart. Just as she was about to collapse, Kuronono skipped over in her micro bikini.

"Ah! Sir Alan! Um, excuse me!" She seemed apologetic. "Um, I'm sorry. The folks in the Shovel Squad have been complaining... 'An earthquake? Is he out of his mind?' 'I love Lady Kuronono, but that's impossible.' 'Even with my love for princesses in micro bikinis, that's impossible.' Stuff like that..."

"Hrm, I see. I'm not sure I understand, but the long and short of it is you're struggling, yeah?"

Odessa felt newly at ease. So the Shovel Squad retained some semblance of human common sense.

Thank goodness. The Kingdom of Darkness is still a country of humans, not demons or worse, shovels.

"Odessa, that's why..." Kuronono turned to her friend and threw a bomb right in her face. "I want you to perform a shovelive with me."

In the background, someone heard a shovel fall off a cliff. Odessa's consciousness fell off a cliff as well.

"And then everyone'll say things like 'All scoop the super serious Lady Odessa!' 'Resistance is love!' 'Red-haired pony-tailed C-cup white bikini is love!' 'My shovel is quivering!' If you perform, they'll be able to do it! Pleeease?"

Odessa's consciousness was fading.

I understand nothing. I know nothing. Well, there is a single thing I understand.

"Hrm, you don't appear to be doing so well. Let me use Shovel Healing on you."

"Thank you so much, Sir Alan!"

As of today, the Kingdom of Darkness is now the Kingdom of Shovels.

PART 41
The Lady Knight Loses Her Best Friend

THE KINGDOM OF DARKNESS was comprised of twelve mountains beneath which lay twelve underground cities.

Odessa had made her way to one such city, the City of White Mythril. There she was supposed to meet Alan's ally Catria, who would share critical information about the revolution. After passing through the extradimensional hole Alan had dug (Odessa didn't even bother to interject anymore), she emerged in a relatively large cave.

A battle between the forces of man and Hell unfolded before her. Multiple winged demons were up against about thirty human warriors.

"Comrades, charge! Let us take back our pride as humans!!!"

Once the human leader delivered her orders, the equally human soldiers smashed headfirst into the demons. The clash of swords and claws filled the cave. Odessa watched this fierce battle for independence from the side.

"Ah... Everyone..." Odessa's eyes widened with hope as tears took shape. The humans were fighting on equal footing with the demons. No, not even equal. They were fighting better.

And...

"They're using swords, not shovels!"

Odessa found herself most touched by this simple fact. She felt weak in the knees as she cried tears of joy. *Even without shovels, we can stand against the demons...!*

"Hm? You with the red hair! Are you all right?!" The dignified, also red-haired female soldier who had been delivering orders rushed over to Odessa.

It was Catria; she was in charge of the liberation front at the City of White Mythril.

Odessa introduced herself and her position, then wiped her eyes. "I must apologize! I was so moved I couldn't help but cry."

"You were moved?"

"Yes...um... The soldiers were fighting demons without shovels, so..."

Catria immediately understood what Odessa was getting at and felt warmth bubbling up within her. *She's like me. This red-haired girl is absolutely just like me. A fellow human standing against the greatest threat to this world, in other words, the shovel!*

Catria grasped Odessa's hands and the two of them shared a moment gazing into each other's eyes.

"It must've been so hard for you, Odessa. Let's take back common sense together!"

"Catria...!"

"From here on out, we're besties!"

Odessa truly felt as though she had found her savior. Her mind, once corrupted by Kuronono and Alan's dual shovels, was finally clearing.

That's right... I'm not the weird one... The shovel is what's weird! Odessa wiped her tears again and stood tall. "Catria! Let me fight with you! Give me a weapon!"

"But of course, Odessa!"

Catria gave an order to one of her underlings and they handed the red-haired revolutionary a weapon. It was a silver spear approximately six feet in length, and its sharp tip filled Odessa with courage.

Yes, that's right! A spear, not a shovel! Not an excavating tool, but a proper weapon!

As she was inspired by the spear in her hand, she noticed

its red handle. Something like that would be extremely useful if one needed to stab the blade into the ground. In fact, it was the sort of handle one might find on a shovel.

Wait...

"What's wrong, Odessa? Are you better with a sword?"

"No, it's not that... It's nothing, Catria!" Odessa shook her head, chasing away her doubts. She then charged the demons with her comrades-in-arms.

I'm just imagining things! I haven't shaken off the brainwashing is all!

She thrust her silver spear forward as if she were piercing through her worries.

SHIIIIIING!

The weapon left behind a silver trail of light as it cut through the flesh of the advancing demons like a knife cutting through butter.

"GAAAAAAAAARGH!"

Amazing! It takes them down so beautifully. This is the true power of a holy spear!

"Don't let your guard down, Odessa! They have potent healing abilities. They'll get up again soon!"

"All right! How can we stop them from regenerating?!"

"Like this!" Catria raised her Holy Knight Blade and swung it toward the ground.

KA-CHOOOOOOOOM!

Catria opened a six-foot-long rectangular hole in the earth and dropped the demons into it.

"Okay! We're sealing them up!"

All of the able-bodied and free soldiers rushed over and stabbed their spears into the ground, shoveling up dirt. The demons were soon buried below, and Catria wiped the sweat off of her brow.

A perfect job, I must admit.

"..."

Odessa watched Catria work in silence. Her expression could best be described as "Should I really point out what just happened?"

Had Odessa noticed something off during their battle with the demons? Catria found herself legitimately bemused.

"Um, Catria...?"

"What's up? Curious about the sealing process?"

"Well, um, I just...this is really hard for me to say..."

"Don't hold back! We're friends who've promised to stand against the shovel together, after all!" Catria's smile was radiant.

That only made Odessa's heart ache further. *Should I really say it? Will I hurt her if I do? And what if I'm just overthinking things...?*

Odessa was lost as to what to do. The approach of

bony footsteps interrupted her dithering. A legion of skeletons marched out of the darkness.

"Looks like there's a demon necromancer among them. Everyone, stand back!"

A new enemy force had arrived. Catria stood at the front of her soldiers and raised her Holy Knight Blade. Everyone watched from behind with bated breath. Catria's entire body emanated a holy silver aura.

At the sight of her, the skeleton army stalled in place.

This is amazing! thought Odessa. Catria had paralyzed the army of undead with her aura alone. She was just like the Holy Knights from all the stories. *I knew it. I knew I was just overthinking things.*

Just as a wave of relief washed over Odessa, causing her to once again tear up, Catria cried out.

"Unholy beasts! BE GONE! HOOOLLLE-YYYYYY!" KA-CHOOOOOOOOM!

The silver beam of energy launched from her weapon disintegrated the skeleton army.

Odessa's tears had stopped. Actually, it felt like time itself had stopped.

"…"

"What's wrong, Odessa?" Catria returned to her new friend only to find her motionless.

What did she just say? She said "holy," right? Yeah,

totally. For sure. It only kinda sounded like "hole." I'm over-thinking this. Plus, even if she did say "hole," that doesn't necessarily mean it has anything to do with shovels. God, I'm losing it. Yup. Catria's my friend and a Holy Knight. She has nothing to do with shovels.

Odessa repeated this last part to herself over and over again until a smile crossed her face.

"Y-you were amazing, Catria! That was incredible holy magic!"

And that was that. Odessa was a kind girl.

"Thanks!" Catria smiled proudly before high-fiving her new friend.

But soon, her expression went stiff. Catria's gaze was fixed down a tunnel, from which a low rumbling could be heard. Even Odessa grew serious. The sound was familiar. When it came to caves, this was the kind of thing you never wanted to hear.

In other words, it was a flash flood. Somewhere, the demons had destroyed a water storage tank.

"Catria, we have to run!"

"It'll be fine, Odessa." Catria smiled confidently and held up her Holy Knight Blade.

That smile gave Odessa an awful sense of déjà vu. It was all too similar. To whom, one might ask? To Alan the miner, of course.

"..."

Just as the light faded from Odessa's eyes, Catria cried out.

"JUSTICE SHREEEEEEEEEEEEEM!"

KA-CHOOOOOOOOOM!

Catria fired all the Holy Shovel Power gathered in her Holy Knight Blade in a single blast. It made a beam approximately four inches in diameter that smashed head-on into the flash flood with an impact that made the ground itself shake. Its momentum cut straight through the raging waters.

By the time the flow of light had ceased, not a single droplet remained.

Cheers erupted from behind Catria.

"All hail Lady Catria!"

"All hail our Holy Knight!"

Heh. Catria turned around with a triumphant smile on her face. "What'd you think of that, Odessa? Awesome, right? That was my Justice Stream!"

"..."

Odessa breathed heavily and prayed for strength. Finally, she spoke. She could no longer keep the truth to herself. "Look, Catria. This is so, so hard for me to say, but..."

"What is it? We're already besties. Tell me what's on your mind!"

Odessa had to tell her. Tell her she didn't actually scream "Justice Stream." But the girl before her had called Odessa her best friend. She was dazzling. And more importantly, Catria was thrilled she'd gotten to perform her duties as a Holy Knight.

"Y-your Justice Stream was so strong!" Odessa lost to Catria's joyful gaze.

"Right?!"

Whatever. We're best friends. It's fine. I'm just going to forget she combined "stream" and "shovel" to make Justice Shreem. It's all going to be okay.

Odessa was a kind girl.

"All right. We've got control of this sector! Time to meet up with the princess!" called Catria.

"The princess?"

"My master. She's leading a separate squad along with Alice. But be careful, Odessa." Catria's expression was most serious. "The princess is dangerous right now. Extremely so. Do not approach her alone."

"Um, what? Catria, you do realize you're speaking of your master right now, yes?"

"She's *dangerous*." Catria swallowed loudly and continued. "The princess is extremely...shovel."

Shovel (adjective).

Odessa's eyes filled with a deep sadness.

"She's *extremely* shovel. That's the only adjective I can think of to describe her. She's like a shovel that's taken human form. Her words in particular are very shovel. Do not approach her without an anti-shovel strategy. I've prepared special earplugs for use against her. They're reverse shovel-shaped so they completely fill your earholes."

"Um, Catria?"

Alas, the knight continued to explain, completely ignoring Odessa's attempts to cut in.

"But even these special earplugs can't completely cancel out the princess's shovel words. And so I came up with the idea of burying myself into the ground; I can use the dirt to cut off any sound, thereby preventing myself from getting brainwashed. If something ever happens, let's promise to bury each other, okay?"

"Look, Catria, this is really, *really* hard for me to say, but..." Odessa could hold back no longer.

I'm so sorry, Catria. But I have to tell you now.

She cleared her throat.

"You've already been completely corrupted by shovels," Odessa said matter-of-factly.

And just like that, Catria gained and lost a best friend within the same day.

PART 42

The Princess Fires a Wave Motion Shovel Blast

BY THE TIME ALAN arrived at the City of White Mythril, Catria's eyes were dead. Upon seeing Alan's shovel, she yelped and shuddered, then shook her head as if to force out some unseen thing. She could be heard whispering to herself, "No...th-that's impossible... I haven't lost to the shovel...I haven't...!"

Tears were rolling down her cheeks. Was she crying? Over some kind of "defeat"?

"Odessa, what happened?"

"Something terribly, terribly difficult..."

"I see..."

Odessa's attitude told Alan she didn't want to talk about it, so he decided to keep his hands off the situation. Anyway, one of Catria's best qualities was how snappily she was able to recover from this sort of thing. She'd be back to normal in no time.

"Then let's catch up with Lithisia."

Lithisia was in the middle of a liberation mission with Alice. According to her regular Shovel Communication report, the mission was going swimmingly.

"But it'll be bad if we let her work on her own for too long," said Alan. "Let's hurry."

"Is something wrong?"

"Absolutely. The entire world could be buried."

"Um, Alan, are you sure you're not talking about yourself?"

"I'm just a miner. But Lithisia isn't just a princess."

"I'm pretty sure that's a lie."

"I promise you I'm not lying."

Odessa followed along after Alan as he made his way through the cave.

She just doesn't know yet, Alan thought.

Indeed. Odessa didn't yet grasp that not only was Lithisia not just a princess, she wasn't even a member of the human race.

Meanwhile, Lithisia and Alice had advanced on the Seat of the Black Iron King. This was both a spot for mining black iron as well as the king's throne room. In other words, it was the deepest point in the entire country.

Of course, this also meant that demons were all over the place.

"Mwa ha ha ha ha! Go forth, my Neo Alice Army!"

The formidable undead army pressed forward. Alice had used her necromancy to summon powered-up skeletons and specters numbering in the tens of thousands. How? Well, she had taken the orbs from the Mage King Farshinal in Rahzelfo and was making great use of them.

Under normal circumstances, the undead stood no chance against demons, but...

"Hee hee hee, I'm amazing! This is a slaughter!"

Alice was on cloud nine as she watched her army charge. They were extremely capable. The skeletons' swords, shining a radiant blue color, were powerful enough to cut through the demons' Hell Breath. Likewise, the specters wielded staffs with brilliant blue auras, and they completely overwhelmed the demons' black magic.

My magic can best the demons of Hell! Hee hee hee, I've gotten stronger since doing battle with Alan. I knew it! I'm not just some naked girl who's only good for being scooped! I'm invincible!

Just then, a voice came from behind.

"Alice! It's about time we recharge our Shovel Power!"

"EEK!"

Alice was invincible to all but Lithisia and her shovel.

"W-we're in the middle of a mission! Get back!"

"Now, now. Don't be like that. If we don't recharge, we're going to lose, shovel!"

"That doesn't make sense!"

Lithisia tilted her head, puzzled. "Without Shovel Power, your 'shoveltons' and 'scoopters' will go back to normal."

"THAT'S NOT WHAT THEY'RE CALLED!"

"Shoveltons" and "scoopters" weren't any kind of undead Alice was familiar with.

"Oh, did you not notice? I strengthened them with my shovel, shovel!"

"How?!"

"What's a few letters in the face of a shovel?"

"You literally just replaced huge chunks of their names!"

This was nuts, but the truth was Lithisia had indeed strengthened Alice's forces. Actually, they were way too strong. Hell, the skeletons were firing off blue beams from their swords like it was no big deal. Alice realized with a sinking feeling that she knew of no skeletons capable of doing such things. But she did know of shovels that could.

"So that's that! Scoopy, scoopy, scoop!"

Lithisia embraced Alice from behind where she sat on her skeletal palanquin. With her own legs, she locked Alice's in place. It was the usual scooping stance.

N-no way! She's seriously going to do this now?! Stop it, stop it, stop it, PLEASE!!!

Lithisia rubbed the undersides of Alice's feet with her silver shovel.

Scoopy, scoopy, scoop!

"EEEEEEEK!"

Scoop, scoop, scoooop!

"SCOOOOOOOOP!!!"

As Alice writhed, her skeleton army grew more and more excited.

"S-stop this at once!!! Why is that shovel so tingly?!"

"Because it's my special 'Aliscoop'!" Lithisia smiled as her silver shovel shone in the light.

"Aliscoop?!"

"It's short for Alice-Exclusive Scooper!"

That didn't explain a thing! Alice tried her best to resist, but as she flailed—the silver shovel fell from Lithisia's grasp and clattered down a crevasse.

CLANK!

"EEEK!"

The shovel tumbled end over end into the Kingdom of Darkness' labyrinthine tunnels.

"Aaaah! My Aliscoop! I have to go get it!" cried Lithisia.

"Haaah, haaah. I'm saved! What a diabolical tool…"

"You're going to be Shovel Punished later!"

"WHY?!"

And so Lithisia went after her Aliscoop, descending deep into the earth and following its presence all the way to a ten-foot-tall metal door. Judging by the layout of the underground, the hole her Aliscoop fell down connected to the room behind this door.

"Haaah, haaah, it's finally over…!" Alice was in tatters after receiving her Shovel Punishment on the way down. Even without her Aliscoop, Lithisia still had her little red shovel.

The princess went to open the grand door but stopped in her tracks. "That's odd…I'm not feeling any Shovel Presence other than the Aliscoop from beyond this door."

"It'd be weirder if you did. There's probably a demon on the other side."

"Even if there was, I'd still feel some kind of Shovel Presence. Did you know all demons have sharp horns on their heads? Their sharpness is a lot like the sharp tip of a shovel. In other words, they're shovels."

"That makes no sense. Don't even bother trying to explain it."

Shovel corruption was spreading even to the demons. The end of the world was nigh.

"Alice, be scoopful."

"But I refuse."

"In the common tongue, that means 'be careful.'"

"If you have to explain it, don't bother saying it in the first place!"

"Absoscooply not (absolutely not)."

Trying to communicate with this princess was more difficult than attempting to reason with a demon.

"That said, I'm also getting a bad feeling about this," Alice admitted. "What do you want to do? Call Alan?"

The miner would arrive in three seconds should they summon him. Even if they didn't, he'd probably turn up if they were in a pinch. But after thinking for a few seconds, Lithisia shook her head.

"No, we're going to do this together."

Conquering the Kingdom of Darkness was one of the tasks required to scoop (read: conquer) the world, as Lithisia had discussed with Alice. Furthermore, there was Catria's solo defeat of the Mage King to consider. As Catria's master, Lithisia was therefore also compelled to prove the power of the shovel she had received from Alan.

"It's scooping time."

"I have no idea what you mean."

It wouldn't be long before Lithisia discovered her choice was absoscooply not the right one.

They had found their way to the second floor of the underground Great Cathedral, a massive space within which the Pleasure Bell that controlled the enslaved demons once hung. Beneath them, the first floor contained an altar, a vase brimming with black liquid, and a shadowy figure.

The figure stood absolutely still, until it groaned with a long and eerie voice, like the sound of wind passing through a hole. It wore a gray robe and held a tin staff with an orb attached to the end, and it emanated an unearthly violet and black aura. Though its form was humanoid, it was certainly no kind of human.

Alice knew exactly what manner of being it was, and on a horribly personal level.

"That's not very shovel, is it?" Lithisia whispered from the second floor as she hid herself behind a pillar.

What exactly was this creature?

"It's not human, demon, angel, or a shovel..." she murmured.

" ... "

"Alice, do you know what... Alice?"

"Ngh...!"

Finally, Lithisia noticed something was off with Alice. The undead king was perfectly still, not even breathing. Yet she was trembling—no, spasming. The creature below had paralyzed her.

Fortunately, it only took Lithisia a few rubs to the bottom of Alice's feet to bring her back.

"EEEEK!"

"It's not very shovel to ignore someone."

Alice raised a rather...compromised voice in response to Lithisia's surprise attack.

"C-could you please stop it? Now's not the time to be messing around!" Alice was no longer frozen, but her expression was deeply serious. "We have to call Alan, now! We don't stand a chance against...*that*!"

The chill running down Alice's neck wouldn't stop.

"I've been trying to call him via Shovel Telepathy, but he's not answering," said Lithisia.

"What?!"

"There's some sort of wall, a really hard wall, between us."

"This is bad! We have to run!" Alice's teeth were chattering. The instincts carved into Alice's very soul were telling her to quake in fear, for before her stood a being she had to avoid at all costs. "That's a god. The real deal 'God of Death and Destruction,' Veknar!"

Veknar, the creator of the Crown of Veknar, the ancient artifact that had given Alice her undead immortality. The god who governed death and destruction. That was this figure's true identity. He usually resided in the extra-dimensional castle Deardol Vectia, so why was he here? What had happened in this place?

"I have to find out..." Alice focused her mental energies.

As the undead king, Alice was capable of looking into scenes of the past by utilizing the lingering grudges in an area.

A blurry vision ran through Alice's mind. Sitting at the altar of the Great Cathedral was a whopper of a horned demon—a demon priest. It was performing some kind of summoning ritual, which explained the vase filled with human blood sitting atop the altar. The demon priest was trying to summon the king of demons.

But something went wrong. After all, Veknar was not the king of demons.

"Come forth, Master!" As the ritual neared its completion, the demon priest cried out.

Clank, clank, clank, plop!

Just as he did, a silver shovel fell from the ceiling straight into the vase. It was the Aliscoop.

"Huh?" The demon priest was confused. But even as he spoke, the vase began to shine, and in the next moment, Alice's vision died as "God" descended upon the land.

Alice's eyes widened and she screamed. "This is our fault?!"

"EEEK!"

"It's the shovel you dropped! That was the catalyst!"

Veknar was one in body and soul with Alice. It made sense that if Alice's personal shovel was used as the catalyst of a summoning spell, Veknar would be called.

This was bad. He was the real deal. They needed to run as soon as possible; if they didn't, they were doomed. Alice could sense this instinctively because Veknar was her, just as she was him.

"!!!"

A voice made direct mental contact with Alice. No, it was more like the voice was overwriting her own. *Why? Lithisia, no! Master. My master...*

"Hrm, you're a part of me. You shall be a temporary body for my resurrection." A cold thing spoke with Alice's voice, but it wasn't her. "You shall not escape."

"Ah..." The light in Alice's eyes faded. *I'm going to vanish. Even after overcoming death, I'm just going to disappear. Of course I am. I exist to become one with my master.*

Alice reached out. She was completely defenseless.

As Alice's arms lifted, Lithisia thrust her shovel into Alice's armpit.

Shoop, shoop, shoop!

"EEEEEEEK!!!"

Alice responded as intended.

"What?" A booming voice snarled from the robed figure below. "A mere vessel escaped from my control? Impossible. Once more!"

SHIIIIIING!

Veknar directed a cold glare up at Alice.

"SCOOP!"

The princess continued to scratch and scoop at Alice's side until the undead king was completely soaked in sweat. The battle for control over Alice's soul was too intense for her young body to handle. All she could do was shake her head in tears.

"NOOO, STOP IT! I'M GOING TO DIEEEEE!"

Veknar watched this with great curiosity. "What was that just now? How fascinating. What have you done to my vessel?"

"Scooped! (Scooped!)"

"Hrm?"

"Scooped! (Scooped! (Scooped!))"

A few seconds passed.

"Event modification, is it? But I don't sense any magic or holy energy. A technique born on the surface, then?" said Veknar.

"S-scoop...!" Sweat droplets beaded on Lithisia's forehead. *This is absoscooply bad.*

Lithisia was scooping repeatedly, but Veknar wouldn't let himself get shoveled (couldn't be shaken). When Alice said he was a god, she meant it in the true shovel sense.

After a few seconds, Lithisia made her decision. "Alice, I'll hold him off, shovel!"

In the meantime, Alice would call for help. This was their only shot at survival.

Alice was leaking all kinds of Alice-juices as Lithisia lifted her up with her shovel. "Wha?!"

"Alice, hurry and get Sir Miner!"

"Eeek?! I'd love to run, but!"

If Veknar called for her, Alice would lose control of her very soul. The only reason she had maintained herself thus far was Lithisia's Shovel Powers (status restoration). (Actually, Alice got the feeling it was less restoration and more like overwriting, but whatever.) Either way, the second Alice left Lithisia's side, she'd be under the god's control.

"Don't worry. I had a feeling this might happen, so I developed a completely autonomous shovel weapon!"

Lithisia whipped out something resembling a leotard. It was a pure angelic white and in Alice's size, but on the inside were thousands of small protruding bits. These weren't tentacles but in fact small shovel heads, in other words, way worse than tentacles—especially as these shovel heads actively sought out Alice's skin.

"!!!"

SHIIIISCOOOOP!

(The sound of Alice's spine quivering in fear.)

"It's a Shovel Suit! Put it on, Alice!"

"No! Absolutely not!" If Alice wore that suit, her soul would be forever lost.

"With this, you can be scooped endlessly even when I'm not around! Come, Alice!" Lithisia held her red shovel in her left hand and the Shovel Suit in her right.

"STOP IIIIIIIT!"

This was a complete disaster.

Amidst the chaos, Veknar finally made his move. "I see, so you're the intermediary. I wonder what will happen once you're gone?"

"Huh?"

"DEATH RAY."

SHA-BAAAAAAAANG!

Veknar fired a beam from his finger. The red shovel in Lithisia's left hand was obliterated.

All sound stopped for Lithisia. It felt like the entire world had ceased to move.

"Huh...?"

Her shovel. The precious shovel she had received from Sir Miner. The shovel, more precious than her life, humanity, or even all the universe...it was gone?

"Now you can't use that technique of yours. This is the end." Veknar pointed his finger at Lithisia.

SHA-BAAAAAAAANG!

This beam was even more fierce than the last.

This is bad...this is really, really bad!

The impact of losing her shovel sped up Princess Lithisia's internal thought processes (as a human). She had dedicated over 99 percent of the resources in her brain to thinking about shovels, and now that it was gone, her former genius-level intellect had kicked back into gear. In other words, she was normally operating at less than 1 percent of her total mental capacity.

What can I do?!

She understood the entirety of her situation. It was bad. The worst, even.

Also, Lithisia recognized that beam of Veknar's. It was the same as the beam Alan once used to destroy the bandits' swords. In other words, she was facing someone on the same level as her Sir Miner—someone capable of breaking the laws of the world. There was no way she could win. She had to run. She had to somehow get Alan's help...

Something strange was happening to Alice.

"Ah..."

Alice's body slowly fell forward. Lithisia nearly fainted as she watched. Alice's once silver form now produced dark energy. She was de-shoveling. The tug-of-war between Veknar and Alice's internal shovel had come to a close. Alice was disappearing.

My belovedly shovely Alice will be no more... Is that really okay? My shovel won't be a shovel anymore... Is that really okay?

"Not..." Lithisia murmured.

"Hrm?"

"Absoscoemply not! I...I am a SHOVEL!" Of course it wasn't okay! That was why Lithisia yelled at the top of her lungs: "CHARGE UP SEQUENCE, ACTIVATE!"

Lithisia held her hands in the shape of a triangle. She had no shovel to call her own, but so what? Everything in this world was a shovel. She had decided she herself was a shovel. She had to be one, lest Alice disappear forever.

I received my shovel from Sir Miner. That's why I am a blade that pierces the very rules of this planet.

Lithisia Power: 120 percent. Safety Systems: all green.

"DIIIIIIIG!"

KA-CHOOOOOOOOM!

"Ha!"

Lithisia fired a beam from the ends of her hands. It was much smaller than Alan's, but it was without a doubt a Wave Motion Shovel Blast. It was a collection of Lithisia's pure energies, fired by Lithisia herself. A weapon to pierce and dig through the rules of the world.

Veknar took the blast head-on.

A moment passed.

"Not bad at all. However, this is just the beginning." Veknar raised his hand. "WORLD OF REFLECTION."

SHINK!

Lithisia's beam was reflected back at her.

"No way?!" As Lithisia watched her own beam career toward her, she recalled Alan had once told her of beings beneath the surface who could reflect the Wave Motion Shovel Blast. That was why he took "safety first" so seriously. *Ah...I'm so sorry, Sir Miner...*

She had failed his teachings. Lithisia couldn't be a shovel. She was a human woman who could do naught but despair over the beam of light advancing on her body.

"DIG!"

KA-CHOOOOOOOOM!

Another beam of light cut through the princess's.

"Huh...?" Lithisia opened her eyes wide and found herself staring up at the back of a man standing before her.

It was the strong, sturdy back of the most dependable man in the world. The man with the shovel. He stood in front of Lithisia, protecting her from Veknar.

"Sorry to keep you waiting."

It was Alan.

"Ah..."

Lithisia gazed at his back with her mouth half-open. She wanted to say something, but no words came out, just a series of sounds. The tears she had been holding back ran freely, blurring her vision. Her emotions overflowed. Her beloved shovel. Her overflowing shovel.

"Leave the rest to me." Alan casually held out his shovel and turned to Veknar. "Even against the divine itself, my shovel won't lose."

Lithisia shed tears. Tears for her savior.

"Who are you?" said Veknar, now facing Alan's shovel.

Veknar didn't let his guard down as Alan shook his head.

"I'm Alan the miner."

"A miner... Ah, yes, I remember hearing of you now." Veknar gave Alan a long hard look of great interest. "A human who overcame their own mortality. I heard tell of you from Asmodeus."

"Enough with the chitchat. Are we doing this or not?"

"Not right now. Much like you, I err on the side of safety first."

"..."

"Feel free to cause as much chaos on the surface as you'd like with my vessel and that little princess of yours." Veknar began to hover in the air, his robes fluttering into darkness. "Hee hee, fascinating. You might very well be able to seize the Pantheon."

"I don't intend to."

"It matters not what you desire. It is your fate." And then Veknar vanished with these final words: "Let me give you one piece of advice... Asmodeus has your treasured orb."

And so the robed Veknar left Alan, Lithisia, and the unconscious Alice behind in the shadows of the Great Cathedral.

"Um, Sir Miner...?"

Alan turned, causing Lithisia's heart to leap. She didn't know what to say to him. Wait, she had to apologize for leaving the battleground and getting in trouble against orders—not to mention getting her precious red shovel destroyed! As a believer and follower of the Holy Shovel Faith, she was ready to be punished with death. That was why she had to apologize first and...

"You have my gratitude. You did well, Lithisia."

"Huh?"

For some reason, Alan thanked her. "It's thanks to you that everyone ended up okay."

"Wh-what?"

These words were entirely unexpected.

"That guy's god-barrier meant I couldn't get a lock on your location. Your Wave Motion Shovel Blast is what let me find you."

"Huh? Um, er, um…"

"You did great, Lithisia."

"Ah…aaauhhhh…"

Sir Miner praised me. I was useful to him at last!

"Ah…scoop…shovel…!"

This truth made Lithisia quite the happy little shovel.

She remained in this delirious state for a solid few minutes, all the way until Catria appeared and found the princess melting with delight, Alice catatonic on the floor in her Shovel Suit, and Alan digging up a barrier to guard against god-tier enemies.

"By the way, Alan, which mountain are we freeing next?" asked Catria.

"We're mostly done, actually. But according to some new intel, it seems the demons took the Purple Orb deep below."

"Oh, right. We're collecting orbs. I forgot about that." Catria was so focused on saving the world from shovels she had lost track of their original objective.

"Which means it's time to go to Hell."

Catria thought for a few seconds before sighing. She was only surprised by the fact that his sentence didn't surprise her in the slightest.

No, the fact that I recognize that means I'm still mostly human.

Catria nodded to herself firmly. Once she got back from Hell, she'd have to have a nice long chat with Odessa so she could regain some of her basic reason.

Her shovel was only just beginning.

PART 43
The Miner Goes to Hell

AND SO THE TRIO of Alan, Lithisia, and Catria headed into the depths of Hell to retrieve the Purple Orb.

First they dropped by the World Tree Castle, where they briefly greeted a happy (and bouncy) Fio, only to tell her that they were going to "drop in on Hell for a sec." They used shovel transmission (skipping while merrily singing about shovels; it's quite fun) to descend the 6,666,666 steps to Hell.

At last, Catria and the others arrived on the creepy, purple-hued plane of Hell.

"So, this is Hell," said Alan.

"Can you not say it like you're some kind of easy-breezy tour guide?!" After screaming, Catria took several steadying breaths.

I'm really here.

Despite being deep below the surface world, there was actually a sky; it was ashen, but it was there. Storm clouds and giant balls of fire roiled above. One ball smashed into the surface overhead, exploding.

I'm actually, really here.

Catria was dizzy. The air was so cold she might freeze, but her skin was so hot she might burn up. Her senses were going crazy. In no way was this a place intended for humans.

"Sir Miner, is this the demons' home base, shovel?" Lithisia, on the other hand, looked perfectly fine. She really had given up her humanity.

"It's one specific demon's home base, to be more accurate. This is an area called 'Baadr,'" Alan explained.

Hell was actually made up of several distinct areas, or dimensions. Baadr was Asmodeus's territory. Notably, this region was thought to be governed with relative order compared to some of the others.

"The person we're looking for should be in the Prison City Dis, which is located at the center of Baadr."

"Should we expect combat?"

Alan had once said he fought a demon lord. Catria could believe him now; there was no way it wasn't true.

"No. We're going to negotiate. My contact can be a bit of a hardass, but they're no idiot."

"You mean there are demons you can actually negotiate with?"

"Well, not with words. But shovels work."

"Amazeshovguage! (Sir Miner's shovel language is as amazing as ever!)" Lithisia was still in the happiest of shovel states. She had received a brand new shovel as a replacement for her old one.

I get what he's saying, but... Catria frowned.

Alan said his contact was Asmodeus, who as far as Catria knew was the demon lord said to have led the army of darkness during the eternal war between the gods, Ragnarök. Asmodeus's magic power had ripped the surface world to pieces. This wasn't the sort of entity you picked a fight with for the fun of it.

Get your head in the game, Catria... She took more steadying breaths. *It's going to be okay. Remember all of the adventures you've been on. The pyramid in the desert, the Deep Sea Shrine, the city in the sky. You survived all of them.*

Catria then grabbed the Holy Knight Blade on her back with her shaking hand and clenched it tightly. This action alone provided her with some semblance of courage, mysteriously enough. *As long as I have this sword, I'll be fine. Even in Hell.*

As Catria put an invincible smile on her face, Lithisia giggled.

"Catria! I see you've finally awoken to the fact that you're the captain of the Holy Shovel Knights!"

"Pardon...?"

What the heck is this shovel talking about?

Lithisia didn't even register as a princess to Catria anymore.

"It's just you look so happy with that in your hands."

Catria turned to look at what she was holding. It wasn't a sword. It was a red shovel Lithisia had sneakily placed there.

"GAAAAH!" Catria panicked and slapped the tool down on the ground.

"Ah! Catria, you mustn't waste a good shovel like that!"

"Haaah, haaah!" Sweat poured down Catria's face as she gripped her Holy Knight Blade for sure this time. *No. No, I'm a Holy Knight. I'm not a Holy Shovel Knight. I made a little mistake, that's all.*

Catria took deep breaths again until she found serenity.

All right, I'm okay. I have my sword.

"Your Highness, I am a Holy Knight. I'm happiest when I'm wielding a sword, not a shovel."

"But that Holy Knight Shovel Blade is 50 percent shovel?"

"It's 100 percent *sword*."

"Enough, you two. We're attracting attention," said Alan.

The pair turned around only to hear a bellowing roar. Incomparably huge skeleton dragons were descending upon them. They were unbelievably large, bigger than even the Red Dragon they had faced in the desert. Worse, there was a whole dang bunch of them. At least ten, likely more. They all brimmed with murderous intent.

"Alan! Didn't you say this place was relatively stable?!"

"Relatively. These guys are just very sensitive to the sound of shovels. If you let your guard down, they attack right away."

Catria's experience as a knight warned her of the degree of imminent danger. Just one skeleton dragon was bad enough. Extremely bad. Its fierce crossfire breath was an inevitability. She had to run.

No! She had to cut down her enemy. She would find a way through this oncoming swarm of death. Catria made her decision in a matter of milliseconds and moved to fire her Justice Stream.

"DIG!"

KA-CHOOOOOOOOM!

But before she could, Alan's Shotgun Wave Motion Shovel Blast pierced Hell's sky. The light blue beam of energy even cut through Hell's lightning, engulfing all of the skeleton dragons. They let out cries of terror as they vanished.

The battle was over in an instant.

"..."

Catria was still holding out her Holy Knight Blade.

Alan somehow felt bad for her. "My apologies, Catria. I had planned to leave at least one for you to take care of, but it'd be a problem if they called for reinforcements."

"Amazshovrabbits! (Amazing! Sir Miner even goes all-out against mere rabbits!)"

"Those weren't rabbits."

"Wow, the shovel is pro animal rights, too!"

Catria still wouldn't move.

"Don't worry," Alan went on. "This is Hell. You'll have plenty of chances to train and...hey?"

Catria *still* wouldn't move. She stared at Alan's shovel. Alan found this strange and took a step closer to her.

WHOOOSH!

Catria swiftly backed up, almost as if she were running away from him.

"What's wrong, Catria? Did you shovel wet yourself?"

"N-no! That's not it, Your Highness!" Catria shook her head as she averted her gaze from Alan's shovel. She clutched her Holy Knight Blade and did everything in her power to erase the thought that had surfaced in her mind for a fraction of a second. *No, no! Absolutely not!*

"Eh? Well, as long as you're good. Let's go. Dis is close."

I will never think "his shovel is so dependable"! Never!

PART 44
The Miner Confesses to the Lady Knight in the Depths of Hell

THE PRISON CITY OF DIS was surrounded by flames. Catria found herself overwhelmed by the sight. Large black towers lined the horizon, and anything resembling a street or a path was made with ashen sand that produced blue flames. Catria felt the heat from the bottom of her shoes. Pretty much everything was on fire, yet amidst all of this, Lithisia was skipping about, merrily singing.

"Sho-vel! Sho-vel!"

She was messed up in the head.

"Catria, you should try Shovel Transmission, too!"

"I refuse."

"It's super fun!"

"I *refuse*."

I'm just going to follow along. I'm not going to skip around in Hell.

"Don't make this harder on yourself, Catria. Get your-self together and use Shovel Transmission." Alan, on the other hand, was walking along the burning Hell sand like it was no big deal.

"Not happening! Princess Lithisia's the only one mad enough to do that!"

"I'm going to have to insist. If you walk around nor-mally in Hell, the flames will roast your very soul."

"Wha?"

Alan explained that Prison City Dis's flames weren't just any old flames, they were Fallen Flames. On contact, a nor-mal human's spirit would be burned to a crisp, causing them to fall into darkness. Using Shovel Transmission allowed one to maintain the integrity of their state of mind and guard against corruption through happily singing about shovels.

During Alan's analysis, Catria felt an uncomfortable jolt in her chest. Her heart was smoldering; it felt like smoke was rising out of her mouth.

"Gah...agh!"

"Catria, this is bad! Hurry and use Shovel Transmission!"

The flames were creeping in on her soul while Princess Lithisia smiled, inviting Catria to the dark side. The lady knight nearly caught herself saying "shovel," but managed to stop at the last second.

No, no, no! Why did I even come on this dangerous

journey in the first place?! To save the world from shovel corruption, right?! Wait, is that really how this all started? Why do I get the feeling I'm wrong... No, either way! I can't afford to let myself lose to the shovel!

"I...won't...lose!"

Think, Catria. Think!

Catria squeezed her Holy Knight Blade. At the end of the day, Shovel Transmission was a technique used to protect oneself from having their heart corrupted. If that was the basic principle, if she focused her powers, there was no rule it had to *directly* involve a shovel!

"Ooooooooh! Blade of mine! Accept my power...!"

Catria continued to clutch her sword. Eventually, her body stopped shaking and she could no longer feel the heat beneath her feet.

"Haaah, haaah..." Catria flashed a fearless smile. *How's that?! I did it! Without a shovel, too!*

Alan couldn't help but be impressed. "Not bad at all, Catria. I'm amazed you managed to devise your own way of guarding your soul from the flames of Hell."

"R-right...?" Joy spread through Catria's heart. She had impressed Alan, and she was terribly proud of that.

"AmazCatriShovelnius! (Amazing! My Catria is a shovel genius!)"

"I'm not a shovel genius."

"But your sword is currently 70 percent shovel."

Slowly, Catria looked down upon the Holy Knight Blade in her hand. Or, what was left of it. It had basically taken the form of a shovel.

"…"

Catria stared at her weapon in shock, then shook her head. She then smashed it vigorously and repeatedly against one of the steel buildings. After a few seconds, it had generally regained its sword form. She wiped the sweat from her forehead and smiled again. "Your Highness, this is no shovel. It's a sword."

"Catria…you've grown so shovely strong."

"It's a sword!" Catria denied the shovel with all of her might, tears in her eyes.

Meanwhile, Alan nodded in satisfaction. He had a warm look in his eyes, almost like that of a father watching over his growing daughter.

And so the three arrived at Asmodeus's palace, Ballad Willnua. It was a terribly strange place. Halls stretched for miles in all directions. Molten steel poured from ceilings as tall as towers. Beneath translucent floor tiles, the stars sprawled in their multitude.

"Space-time is falling apart, melted by the flames," Alan explained. "In other words, don't try digging up the floor here. You'll fall into a distortion of space-time."

"You're the only one who'd try that."

"Scoopty, scoop! Underscooped!" The princess replied as she sang and skipped along.

Catria sighed. Even in this haunting, fairy tale-like place, these two were the same as usual. Being scared would just make her look like an idiot.

"This is it. Keep your guard up," said Alan as he stopped in his tracks. A colossal steel gate awaited them at the end of the hall. As they stood before it, it slowly opened with a boneshaking rumble.

Before them lay the throne room. A long red carpet led into it, and on both sides of the carpet were hundreds of demons standing in a line. But what really caught Catria's attention was the thing sitting on the throne at the center of it all.

It was a girl, almost completely naked, with wavy silver hair and bone-white skin. She looked to be about half as tall as Catria.

"Hrmph, I was wondering who would have the gall to visit."

However, the second Catria met the girl's eyes, her blood became sluggish with fear. It was as if the thing before her could see into her very soul. She couldn't stop shaking. With every quaking cell in her being, the lady knight knew this was the demon lord Asmodeus.

As for Asmodeus, she chuckled.

"It's been three hundred years. I welcome you, Alan the miner." Asmodeus rose to her feet, and she spoke in a voice that seemed to rumble directly within the mind. "What brings you to my palace, shovel?"

"You too?!" Catria interjected with everything she had. *Give me back my sense of danger!*

"No worries, Catria," said Alan. "I'm just using my shovel to automatically translate her thoughts."

"Then there's a critical flaw in your automatic translation system! I feel bad for the demons!"

"You have quite the mouth on you, Shovel Follower of the Miner."

"Excuse me?! I am no follower, I'm...!"

Asmodeus turned her gaze on Catria. It was a piercing gaze that threatened to simultaneously suck out and pulverize Catria's soul. Catria couldn't squeeze out the least bit of sound.

This is bad. She's bad. She's just like Alan before he fires his Wave Motion Shovel Blast.

Then Catria wrapped her hand around her sword, regaining her senses. "I'm...no...follower!"

If this being was anything like Alan, she could overcome them, too!

"Oho!" Asmodeus's eyes flared and she cackled at the lady knight. "Miner Alan! Shoveltastic! A mere human managed to push back against my aura!"

"Catria's no mere human. She's exceptional."

"AmazDemonShovgenius! (Amazing! Catria's such a shovel genius that she's even impressed a great demon!)" Lithisia joyfully bounced about using Shovel Transmission.

Meanwhile, Asmodeus stared long and hard at the princess. She looked vaguely uncomfortable. "Miner Alan, what is that? Is it a person? A shovel?"

"Shovel! (If I had to pick one, I'd say shovel!)"

"Humans truly are fascinating. She possesses the presence of both a human and a shovel."

"Shovel (Humans can't really exist without being shovel)."

"And this one is capable of pushing back against my aura as well. Incomprehensible."

"Shovel (It's the blessing of the shovel.)."

Princess Lithisia had come face-to-face with a similar being not too long ago. She wouldn't budge this time. Asmodeus stared at her with great curiosity.

"It's about time we get to the point. Asmodeus." But there was only one thing on Alan's mind: the return of

the Purple Orb, which had begun as a treasure he exca-
vated himself.

"..."

Asmodeus closed her eyes for a moment and listened
to Alan's case in silence. When at last she spoke, she said,
"Here are my conditions. I'll give you the orb, but in
return, I request a shovel."

An inconceivable response.

"Alan, your translator is busted. Fix it."

"No, it's working just fine. She really did just say she
wants a shovel."

Even a great demon's consciousness had been corrupted by the shovel?

"Then just give them one. You have a bunch on you,
right?" asked Catria.

"I can't. The shovel Asmodeus wants is..."

"Her." Asmodeus pointed at Catria.

An indescribable terror flooded the lady knight.

"Or perhaps, her." Asmodeus then pointed to Lithisia.
She was eyeing both women. It didn't take long to understand what she was implying. "I have a great number of
underlings, but I have no Shovel Underlings. Not yet."

A moment of silence passed. Well, silence other than
Asmodeus as she cackled gleefully. "I quite want one now.
Miner Alan, what is your answer?"

The eyes of the demons lining the throne room glowed red. If Alan said no, they'd attack.

A flood of thoughts rushed through Catria's mind all at once. Could Alan win? Normally she could state with confidence that he had any situation in the bag, but this time, their opponent was something else. Alan had told Catria that when he did battle with the King of Hell, Demogorgon, it was a fierce struggle. Furthermore, Asmodeus was a demon lord on her own turf, meaning she had the homefield advantage.

Plus, if this was an opponent Alan could easily beat, would he have needed to negotiate in the first place? Which meant...

Just as Catria stumbled upon the dire truth of the situation, Lithisia stepped forward.

"You mustn't!"

"Shovel?!"

Catria forcibly pulled the princess back and hurriedly covered her mouth. Lithisia glared at the knight in protest, but Catria didn't care. Regardless of the current circumstances, Lithisia was still a princess. Even if she had thrown away her humanity to become a shovel, Catria would be a failure of a knight if she let Lithisia sacrifice herself.

"Grrr! Shovel! (Catria, stop it! I'm going to shovel you!)"

"I'm sorry, Your Highness, but I can't let you do this." Catria gripped her Holy Knight Blade and stepped forward herself.

Her heart thudded, but not with fear. Her adrenaline was surging because of the upcoming battle. Catria had no intention of becoming an underling for a demon. She might hand herself over now, but she would remain vigilant for any opening that would allow her to destroy that *thing* from the inside. This would be no easy task, but the Holy Knight Blade in her hand gave her courage.

"Wait, Catria. Don't be hasty," Alan said.

But Catria did not wait.

"Alan, I leave the princess in your hands." Catria pushed Lithisia into Alan's arms. Her heart felt refreshed. A smile formed on her face.

But why?

In a heady moment, Catria realized the answer. *At the end of the day, I guess I just wanted to catch him off guard, just once.*

"Asmodeus. I understand your request. I, Holy Knight Catria..."

Shall become your underling.

But just as she was about to finish, Catria found her feet buried in the dirt. This caused her to fall forward and smack her forehead against the floor. It seriously hurt.

"GAAAAAH!"

"I told you not to be hasty," said Alan. "I dug a trap hole there."

"WHY?!"

"As prep for our battle, of course."

Asmodeus's eyebrow moved slightly. Catria twitched as well.

You mean he planned on fighting this thing all along? The reason he didn't take action was because he was making preparations?!

"No, whoa, wait!" said Catria. "I was just gonna pretend to be their underling, not...!"

"You idiot. As if I could ever let you do something that dangerous."

"Better than having the princess do it!"

"I'm not about to make comparisons. You're both equally important to me."

Catria froze. *Er, wait, what did he just say?*

"Miner Alan, will you not give me one of your shovels?" asked Asmodeus.

"I refuse." Alan bluntly denied Asmodeus's request and stood in front of Catria and Lithisia. "It's my job to protect Lithisia. I promised to save her country in exchange for her shoveling for me. She even went so far as to offer herself up to the shovel for that promise."

"Er, Sir Miner?!"

"That's why it's my responsibility to watch over her until the very end."

Lithisia's cheeks nearly exploded as they turned bright pink. The shock from hearing him say "it's my responsibility" was too much for her, and she was now producing shovel juices from all kinds of places. Alan wasn't about to be distracted by this, however.

"And you, Catria. It's my job to raise you. You keep picking up my techniques with incredible speed. Starting with the Wave Motion Shovel Blast, just showing you the Shovel Basics is enough for you to learn them on your own. You're even coming up with your own techniques."

"H-hold on! Wait! What are you...?!"

"Catria, you're like a gold vein of pure talent. That's why...I want to mine everything you have."

A moment of silence settled on the room. Catria couldn't breathe. All she could do was open and close her mouth.

What are you saying, you nut job?! I haven't picked up any shovel techniques! I haven't made any, either!

But she couldn't voice her protests. The last bit about mining everything she had just kept repeating over and over in her head.

She was going to be mined. Catria. Everything.

"?!?!?!"

Aaaaaaaaahhhhhhhh!!! The words wouldn't come out. She felt hot. Her cheeks and chest and all sorts of other places were on fire. *What are you, what are you, what are you saying?!?!*

"Ah, jeez! Ah, jeez! Ah, jeeeeeez!!!!"

You can't just go and say stuff like that to women! You damn natural-born shovel gigolo!

"What's wrong, Catria? Get yourself together. Prepare for battle."

"How can I get myself together, you big, dumb, idiot?!" Catria's heart was racing a mile a minute, and the tears wouldn't stop. Neither would her runny nose.

Damnit, damnit, damnit! This can't be! This is total BS!

"ARRRRGGGGHHHH!" Catria put her hands over her chest and tried to calm her heartbeat.

"Hee hee, Miner Alan. You have quite the shovels on hand."

"I'm not a goddamn shovel!"

"The fact that you're saying that with tears in your eyes already shows just how shovel you are, Shovel Knight." Asmodeus laughed delightedly.

No, no! This can't be! These aren't shovel feelings!

But the pitter-patter in her heart just wouldn't stop.

Alice's Alisquirrshovel Rough

THIS IS A TALE of the time Catria came to the garden at the World Tree Castle in search of Princess Lithisia.

"Your Highness, it's time to eat... What is that?"

Something was walking along the ground. That something was a nude young woman with a large, white, curled up tail extending from her butt.

"This is Alisquirrel!" Lithisia answered confidently.

Catria was at a loss. "Why are you making Alice dress like a squirrel?"

"Catria, I discovered something shovecredible."

Catria regretted asking, but it was too late.

"Squirrels have a really strong compatibility with shovels. Think about it! Both words start with an 's'! And if you squint real hard and flip it upside down, a 'q' kind of resembles the letter 'h'! They're basically one and the same! And then when you pronounce 'Alice,' it sounds like she has an 's' at the end of her name! Put them together, and BAM, they match one hundred percent! This is a shovecredible discovery!"

Not only was Lithisia's explanation overly complex, it was also complete nonsense. If Catria dared to ask any further questions, it was likely she'd step on a landmine.

"This discovery will bring world peace to our planet!"

"If that's the case, I'd rather this planet get destroyed."

"Catria, I'm being completely serious. When Alice is dressed like that, she acts like a squirrel. When people see her acting like a little woodland animal, they won't be able to avoid being filled with joy, and thus we will bring about world peace."

"Isn't that just brainwashing? Sounds kind of horrific, to be frank."

And poor, poor Alice. I really do have to protect humanity.

Just then, Alice walked a few steps, then crouched down and dug at the ground with a little silver shovel.

"Haaah, wrong spot again. Where are my snacks?"

A squirrel burying its food, huh? Eventually, Alice's little shovel clinked against something.

"Ooooh! Here they are! Finally! My candies!"

Alice filled her cheeks with the candy she dug up, a glowing expression on her face.

"They're so tasty!" she said, her tail waving in the air.

Catria stared at this blonde, naked girl (with tail). Eventually, she cracked a smile.

"See?" Lithisia grinned.

"Nngh?! N-no, this isn't what it looks like, Your Highness!"

But Catria couldn't look away from Alice (Alisquirrel). Unfortunately, Alisquirrel (so cute) might actually bring peace to the world.

Afterword

HEYO, Yasohachi Tsuchise here. Volume 3. Yipeeee (insert happy sounds here)!

Ignoring the situation as of late, I'd like to talk about transportation methods in fantasy stories.

In Volume 3, our heroes cross the great ocean, find themselves in the sky, and even journey down into Hell. It's in these "unknown places" and the way to travel to them that I feel the fantastical resides. Mermaid kisses, pegasi, gates to the underworld; all of them are tremendously fantastic.

And since I believe that shovels are also an aspect of fantasy, I wanted to add it in as a potential method of transportation. After thinking on it for a few days, the answer I arrived at was the Shovel Home Run.

Home runs fly a colossal distance, so they can be used for transportation. And since Alan was modeled after Ichiro, and as bats and shovels are both primarily made of wood, I felt that home runs and shovels had a high level of compatibility. I'm going to work hard from here on out to make sure that home runs are used as a means of transportation.

And now some words of gratitude.

Hagure Yuuki-sensei, and my editor...you've both done so much for me that I can't even put it into words anymore. I'm truly, truly a fortunate little shovel. I'd also like to express my gratitude to Renji Fukuhara-sensei who is in charge of the manga adaptation. You made the bandit leader the cutest in the world, and everyone needs to read it. I'm truly grateful.

This has been Yasohachi Tsuchise. Catch you all later, shovel (greeting)!